Kathleen Pope, firefighter turned EMT and now flying with the Minnesota Highway Patrol's Flight Section, and her wife, Belladonna, a business woman who moved to St. Paul four years ago. Up until now the couple had experienced a fairy-tale, whirlwind courtship and a carefree life. All that was about to change. The helicopter that Kathleen is flying in loses power and hits a power line upon takeoff just after loading an accident victim two hours north of Minneapolis-St. Paul. At the very beginning Bella is notified that her wife has been in an accident. From the very first page, Bella and Kathleen have to deal with the exposed, cold, raw, and ugly emotions and physical difficulties that are the down side of even the most blessed lives that everyone lives. The processes and heartaches that are involved when going through terrific tragedies of injuries and deaths are not simple and are not something that are navigated in a single instant.

Follow the lives of Kathleen and Bella from the book, "Falling Into Fire" in this exciting and dramatic sequel. Much like our own lives, we are reminded that nothing is for certain, nothing is written in stone; everything in our lives no matter how perfect it may seem in this moment can change in the blink of an eye.

A HOLLYANNE WEAVER NOVEL

Other Titles by HollyAnne Weaver:

**LEAVING AFGHANISTAN BEHIND
THE PLAID SKIRT
AFTER SASHA
COMING OF AGE
FALLING INTO FIRE**

National Suicide Prevention Lifeline
https://suicidepreventionlifeline.org/
Call 1-800-273-8255
(Veterans, Press **#1** After Connecting!
Or Text to **838255)**

YESTERDAY OVER 20 VETERANS WERE LOST TO SUICIDE.

According to the best study we have right now, each day over 20 veterans take their own lives. But together we can win the war against veteran suicide. Join #Mission22 to let our vets know they have an army behind them.

http://www.mission22.com/#ourcause

HOLLYANNE WEAVER

FURTHER

INTO FIRE

Copyright © September 2018
by HollyAnne Weaver
Published by Shadoe Publishing

ISBN-13: 978-1727258202
ISBN-10: 1727258207

Copyright © September 2018 by HollyAnne Weaver

All rights reserved. No part of this book may be reproduced, stored in a retrieval system or transmitted in any form or by any means without the prior written permission of HollyAnne Weaver or Shadoe Publishing, LLC, except by a reviewer who may quote brief passages in a review to be printed in a newspaper, magazine, or journal.

HollyAnne Weaver is available for comments at hollyanneweaver618@gmail.com and https://hollyanneweaver.wordpress.com as well as on Facebook, or on Twitter @HAWeaver618. Check out her new website at www.hollyanneweaver.com if you would like to follow to find out about stories and books releases or check with www.ShadoePublishing.com or http://ShadoePublishing.wordpress.com/.

www.shadoepublishing.com

ShadoePublishing@gmail.com

Shadoe Publishing, LLC is a United States of America company

Cover by: Cover design for this book was the brainchild of Marie Sterling. Thank you so very much!

FURTHER INTO FIRE

PUBLISHER'S NOTE

This is a work of fiction. Names, characters, places, and incidents are the product of the author's imagination or are used fictitiously, and any resemblance to actual persons, living or dead, business establishments, events, or locales is entirely coincidental.

The publisher does not have any control over and does not assume any responsibility for author or third-party Web sites or their content.

FURTHER INTO FIRE

I don't remember what I was dreaming, but I was definitely having a dream. I looked up at the large digital display on the clock. Until my dying day I'll remember the time: two twenty-seven a.m. The doorbell was ringing again. I had some vague recollection it had already rung. That was followed by heavy knocking on the front door. It startled me plenty, and at first, I wasn't sure whether to answer it or call Pops, my father-in-law, who was a detective lieutenant for the St. Paul Police Department. I moved to the top of the stairs and nearly died in my tracks when I saw the red and blue flashing lights showing through the curtains of the front window. Barely able to breathe, I ran down the stairs, unlocked the door, and yanked it open.

"Bella Pope?" asked the patrolman.
"Yes? What's happened? Is it Kathleen?"
"I'm very sorry, ma'am, but there's been an accident."
"What's going on? What's happened? Where is Kathleen?"
"Can we step inside for a moment?"
"Oh, I'm terribly sorry. Of course. Come in."
I moved out of the way and showed the patrolman to the couch with my outstretched hand. He chose not to sit, instead speaking to me.
"Perhaps it's better if you sit down, ma'am."
"Tell me she's alive! Tell me she's okay!" I nearly screamed at him.
"There was an accident tonight as they were taking off from a crash site about one hundred twenty miles northeast of St. Paul. The pilot managed to radio they were losing power just before the hospital and dispatch both lost radio contact with the aircraft. They hit a low-lying

transmission line, flipping the helicopter over and causing it to catastrophically fail."

"You haven't told me a goddamned thing! I asked you if Kathleen is still alive!"

"Yes, ma'am, she is. She is in extremely critical condition currently and is in surgery at the Hennepin County Medical Center in Minneapolis. One of the pilots, your wife, and the patient that was being transported are all at various hospitals depending on where the other Life Flights came from. Unfortunately, the other pilot was killed in the crash."

"Let me get my coat and purse, and I'll drive over immediately," I yelped.

"Ma'am, isn't there somebody that can drive you? It would be better. I don't think you're in the best frame of mind to be driving right now."

"I'll call my father-in-law. He can probably drive me…or my mother-in-law."

"I'll wait here with you, so you won't be alone, if you'd like."

"Um, okay, sure. Let me get my phone."

I went into the kitchen and picked up the cordless phone, returned to the living room, and sat on the front edge of the easy chair.

"Hello? Pops? Pops?"

❄ ❄ ❄

I came apart. I cried like a two-year-old who'd fallen and scraped both knees. I dropped the phone and leaned over the side of the chair, unable to do anything, just holding my hands over my head and sobbing. The patrolman picked up the phone for me.

"Hello? Yes, sir. This is Keith Dugan with the Minnesota State Patrol. Your daughter would be Kathleen Pope?"

"Yes. Is something wrong?"

"Sir, the helicopter she was flying in tonight was involved in an accident upon takeoff after developing some sort of problem. As I've told Bella, Kathleen is at the Hennepin County Medical Center in extremely critical condition. I've suggested to Bella that she get a ride instead of driving herself. She's really not in any condition to drive, in my estimation…."

"Tell her I'll be there in fifteen minutes or less. Would you stay with her until then?"

"I've already offered. I'll see you in a few minutes, sir."

Patrolman Dugan came over and stood inches away from me, very proper and stiff as a board. He was rock solid while I couldn't be. He reached over to the side table and picked up the box of tissues and handed them to me. I took them, pulled several out, but didn't use them; I was staring into space by then. Fortunately, the wait for Pops was very short. The door opened, and Pops and Kathleen's stepmom, Martha, came into the house.

"Get up and get dressed. We'll drive you over there and help you with anything you need, okay?" Martha asked, lovingly.

I nodded weakly but said nothing, tears streaming down my cheeks. Martha took me by one arm, helped me up, and led me upstairs. She helped me get dressed. For the moment, all I could think of were Kathleen's sweat suits, a whole drawer full and more in the closet. I pulled out a pair that were navy with the crest of the St. Paul Fire & Rescue and the name running down the right leg in huge yellow letters. Martha went into our bathroom and grabbed a few things from the counter, throwing them into her oversized purse. She sat me on the bed and pulled my feet up, putting my running shoes on, then lacing them. Finally, we headed out.

In the car on the way over to the hospital, Pops talked a little, trying to break some of the tension.

"Patrolman Dugan? His father is retired now, but I used to work with him. I thought it might be him. Not too awful many Dugans here. Funny how life has all these little networks of people, who know people, who are related to people, who have friends that are shared–"

"Kevin, will you just drive and be quiet?" asked Martha.

Pops stopped talking. Frankly, I liked it better when he was talking. I just sat there in the back of the car, staring off into space, stunned to my core. You read about fairytale lives. Kathleen and I had that...up until now. Meeting. Getting married within weeks. Being oh so happy the last three years. The biggest thing we ever fought over was how I wasn't taking good enough care of myself, or what we were going to have for dinner that night, or something totally inane. I wasn't prepared for this at all. Finally, we pulled into the drop off, and Pops let me and Martha out. We went inside to the information desk and asked for the surgical waiting room. I had to give them Kathleen's name to get the information, but then, he gave me the room number and directions on how to get there. At first, I was going to wait for Pops, but I just couldn't.

"You go ahead, dear, and I'll bring Kevin when he gets in."

I gave her a hug and went tearing down the hall to find the right room. I finally found the nurse's desk in front and went up to get a status update.

"May I help you?" asked the nurse seated behind the counter.

"Yes, I'm here for Kathleen Pope. Is there somebody who can tell me how she's doing? What they're doing with her? Anything?"

"Are you family?"

"Yes, I'm her wife."

There was about a two- or three-second pause, where the nurse just stared at me. I immediately flew into a rage that was surely exacerbated by my current state of anxiety.

"Yes, I'm gay, and Kathleen is my wife! Can you tell me something, or do you need to get up off your little ass and find me somebody that can?" I yelled at her.

"If you'll give me just a moment, the computer is refreshing. As soon as it finishes, I'll look it up and tell you…" she said, glaring at me.

Screw her and her feelings. I wasn't in any mood for anti-gay, homophobic bullshit from anyone. Not now. Not here.

"She was admitted approximately forty-five minutes ago. She was admitted with severe internal injuries, some broken bones, and it looks like she's still in the operating room. She may well be in there for a long time with the severity of her injuries."

"I want to talk to somebody that can tell me exactly what's wrong with her and what has to be done."

"Ma'am, unfortunately, the information you want is being determined by the people who are caring for her right now. They'll be able to determine the extent of her injuries, what needs to be addressed, and develop a plan of action to remediate all those issues. So, please, have a seat in our waiting room. There are also several couches in there where you can lay down if you wish. I can get you a pillow and a blanket, if you'd like. There's coffee, tea, and a couple of vending machines for sodas and snacks. Unfortunately, our cafeteria and snack bar are closed at this hour."

"All right. Um…I'm…I…I didn't mean to yell at you. I hope you don't think badly of me," I managed as I started breaking down all over again.

"Not at all. I understand that most of what comes out of people here is from tons of stress. Believe me, I've been on your side of the desk before, and I don't mind you being gay, really. I'm sorry if I gave you that impression. I guess I'm just not used to someone as beautiful as you being gay, if that makes any sense?"

"I know. It's a common misconception. But we're working on educating the public."

"If you decide you'd like a pillow or a blanket just come up and let me know, and I'll have someone bring you one. As soon as we have any word, somebody will come talk to you."

"Thank you very much."

Just as I finished talking to the nurse, Pops and Martha walked up behind me, asking if there was any word yet.

"Not a word. Just that she's in surgery. Don't know for how long, don't even know if they'll be able to save her. No word at all, nothing. Only that she has multiple broken bones only God knows where and internal injuries, but I don't have any idea other than it's really bad. I hate this. I just hate this!"

"I know you do, dear," Martha said, putting her arm around me.

"Come on, Bells. Come sit down with me and Martha."

"Pops?"

"Yeah?"

"I like it when you call me that. It makes us seem more like…family."

"Oh, baby, we *are* family! You should know that by now. We're all in this together," he said, giving me one of his signature bear hugs.

It was almost three hours before we heard any word at all. Finally, somebody wearing scrubs, foot covers, a disposable hat, and a surgical mask pulled down around her neck came out and addressed us.

"Is there anybody here for Kathleen Pope?" she called out.

I jumped up quickly, throwing my arm up in the air.

"How is she? Is she going to be okay?"

"My name is Dr. Mei-li Chen. I'm one of three doctors working on Kathleen. We also have two more people coming in, both orthopedic surgeons, to address her skeletal issues once we're at that point. For now, though, I can give you a little bit of information. First off, she's been very badly hurt. Fortunately, there was no fire in the crash, just physical damage, so that's a good thing. No burns. Her right lung was punctured and was re-inflated on the flight here. Her belly was distended when we got her, indicating lots of internal bleeding. We immediately opened her up to drain the blood and did exploratory surgery to find the source of the bleeding and stop it. We removed her spleen to help with that. We also found that her appendix had ruptured from the force of the crash, so we removed that as well. As it is, we have given her four pints of blood as well as clotting factor and platelets."

Dr. Chen hung her head.

"What is it?" I asked.

"We also had to remove her right ovary; it was badly damaged. Her uterus had some tearing, but that was repaired, and we hope that it won't have any lasting effect. We hope it won't affect her ability to have children in the future, but there are no guarantees. And she's going to have some serious scarring in her lower abdominal region. When she was recovered from the accident scene, she had part of a bracket from the aircraft embedded in her belly. We're still not sure about her kidneys, but we should know more within a couple of days based on blood in her urine, output volume, and a few tests. She's got a terrifically well-developed body. If she didn't have a tremendous wall of muscle tissue, I think the abdominal laceration alone would have killed her. I don't want to give you false hope at this point. It's still way too early to tell how she'll respond to all her treatments. In addition, we don't know yet if there are any brain injuries. We do have reaction from her pupils, so that's a fantastic sign, but it's not a perfect measure by any means. She will also have to deal with a broken right femur and a broken left lower arm and wrist. Not to mention, she has several fractures in her facial bones, but those appear to be superficial. They are going to be terribly bruised and look like hell, but that will be the least of her worries. There was no major shift of bone or tissue. Still, there could be ligament and tendon damage all over her arms and legs and many other places. We just don't know yet."

I couldn't take it all in. Kathleen was the strongest person I'd ever met in my life, both physically and mentally. I started moving backwards into the wall, collapsing toward the floor, still staring off into space. Pops immediately grabbed me to keep me from falling all the way down.

"I wish there was more I could tell you now, but she's getting the best care we can give her. We'll let you know more as we have updates," Dr. Chen said.

"Thank you, ma'am. We do appreciate what you and the people on your team are doing," Pops said, offering his hand to the doctor.

She returned his handshake and nodded her head before turning around and going back into the surgery area.

Pops and Martha each took one arm and led me back to the waiting lounge, sitting on one of the couches. Then, Pops walked over to the canteen area on the side, bringing back two paper cups. He handed me one of them.

"Two sugars, two creams, if memory serves?"

I nodded my head. I just couldn't talk. I felt utterly and totally helpless. And we still weren't sure whether Kathleen would live or die. Live or die, I repeated inside my head. Live or die. I started crying again, quietly. I was shaking, tears falling from my cheeks onto my shirt. Pops took my cup and put it on the table at the end of the couch, so I wouldn't spill it.

"Come on. Take a walk with me," Pops said, putting his hand out for me and picking up my purse.

"I want to be here if there is any more news."

"This won't take long. Trust me. Martha, call me on my cell if there's anything new. I'm going to take a little trip with Bells, okay?"

"Sure, you two go ahead. There's no sense in all of us just sitting here waiting. She's so badly hurt, it could be hours before we know much. In the meanwhile, I'll just say a few prayers."

In the three or so years that I've known Martha, I've come to learn that she is so much more than Kathleen led me to believe. Kathleen has really gotten closer to her for the first time in her life as well. We started walking down a few corridors, randomly, I thought. Eventually we wound up at the hospital's internal entrance to the emergency room. Pops walked me over to a chair and had me sit down. He went up to the window, pulled out his badge, showed it to the intake specialist, and pointed to me. The specialist nodded his head. Pops waved me over with his hand. I got up, went to the desk, and sat down.

"Your name, please?"

"Why?"

"I need your name if we're going to see you, ma'am."

I looked up at Pops.

"Why do they need to see me?"

"Belladonna Pope," Pops said for me.

I just sat there, confused.

"Birthdate?"

"October 17th, 1989," Pops continued to answer for me.

"Do you have insurance?"

"Yes, she does," Pops said, pulling my billfold out of my purse and handing it to me.

I pulled out my driver's license for proof of identity and my insurance card and handed it to the man.

"Please take a seat back over there on the left, and we'll call you as soon as we can."

"Thank you," Pops told him, then led me back to the seats.

"I know I'm being stupid, but why are we here?"

"Just trust me, my Bells. Okay?"

I nodded, then lay my head down on his chest while he put his big bear arm around me, hugging me. It took about thirty minutes for them to finally call me. We went back into a small cubicle where a triage nurse took more information. He was the first thing that I'd focused on in hours. I thought he was ruggedly handsome, sort of like my brother. My brother is a bit of an ass and completely misguided most of the time, but he's handsome, and deep down I love him.

"What are you being seen for tonight?"

Pops described the situation and told him that I wasn't holding up too well. He said I needed to see a doctor for something to help with the anxiety.

"Pops, I think I can handle this. I'm a grown-up, you know?"

"Yeah, I know, but so far tonight, you haven't looked much like it. Now, you want to answer the rest of his questions, or do you want me to?"

"I'll answer."

"Fine. Are you allergic to any medications?"

"Cefaclor," I replied.

"Have you been seen here before?"

"I don't know. Doesn't your computer show that?"

"Shhh. Bella, he's only trying to help."

"I'm sorry. You're the third person I've taken my frustration out on tonight. Please, please, forgive me. I'm not usually like this. Really."

"Don't worry about it. I understand."

"Still, there's no excuse. No, I've never been here before. I've only been to St. Joseph's here in the Twin Cities."

He asked about twenty more questions, then had me sign two papers. When that was completed, he put a band on my wrist containing my name, birthdate, and a barcode. He also put on a band that had Cefaclor printed on it in fluorescent red, showing my allergy. Once again, we went to the waiting area. Pops called Martha to check in. Of course, no movement. A very few minutes later they called my name again, and I was taken back to a room. Within fifteen minutes, they'd given me a 10-mg shot of Lorazepam and put me in a wheelchair. An aide came in to push me back to the OR waiting lounge, but Pops said he'd do it, and we returned to find Martha sitting almost exactly as she had been, holding a cup of coffee, her ankles crossed, and her purse under one elbow. Pops left me in the wheelchair for the moment. Martha got up, set her cup down, dug around in her purse, and brought out my brush—one of the items she'd collected from my bathroom. She took about ten minutes to tenderly brush my hair. Then she pulled out some lip gloss and redid my mouth. Finally, she managed to come up with some eye shadow and gave me a little color. Not too much, just enough so I didn't look like the undead.

"There. All better."

"Thanks, Mom."

"Don't mention it. I also managed to get in more than a few prayers while sitting here waiting."

"You know what they said during the Second World War, don't you? 'There are no atheists in foxholes.' I'm not that religious, but I am spiritual. I've already managed to make a few promises to God tonight, if he would just give me back my Kathleen."

She scooted over closer to me and took my hand in hers. We sat there while the medication they'd given me started working its magic. Martha moved over to a chair. Pops picked me up and laid me down on the couch, then went to the nurses' station to ask for a blanket. Within minutes, a nurse brought out three pillows and three blankets, one for each of us. I figured out later, it was still only about five thirty or six in the morning.

I took my phone out of my purse and called my dad.

"Hello? Bella?" he answered.

"Daddy? Kathleen's in the hospital. Her helicopter was in an accident. She's...She's...Oh, Daddy, I might lose her," I said, then I broke down sobbing, nearly dropping the phone.

Pops reached over and took the phone from me.

"Hello, Steven? This is Kevin. We're here at HCMC. Kathleen is in bad shape. She's got a broken leg and radius as well as some facial bones, but the real story is her internal injuries. She's nowhere near out of the woods. At this point, it's pretty grim. They're not even giving us a favorable."

"Damn. Well, thanks for calling. I appreciate it. Keep us updated as you hear anything else, would you?"

"We will. Bye now."

❀ ❀ ❀

"Bella? Bella? Can you wake up? Belladonna?"

I felt someone shaking me gently and heard a voice, but I couldn't tell whose. Gradually, I started coming back to life. It was Martha.

"Bella, the doctor is here. She wants to give us an update."

I looked around me. There was a large picture window at the back of the waiting room, and it was daylight. Not just barely dawn but real daylight.

"Dr. Chen. You're still here?" I asked.

"Well, not for much longer," she laughed.

I smiled at her and stretched. The Lorazepam had knocked me on my butt big time.

"So, here is where we are. We have movement in both feet. We have movement in both hands. So, we know that any damage to the spinal cord is probably, and again, probably, inconsequential. Kathleen has seventeen broken bones: ribs, left arm, left wrist, right leg, six in her face, and her right little toe. There's no more bleeding. We've got that all stopped. In all, she has one hundred eleven internal stitches, which will dissolve by themselves. She also has over two hundred stitches and Steri-Strips externally. To immobilize her left ulna and radius, she's in a halo. Do you know what that is?"

All three of us nodded that we did.

"She'll be in that for probably eight to ten weeks. Her right leg is in a normal cast. Her face is a different matter. She'll be in a cast for that, but it will be something solid in front with elastic from behind. It's to be taken off *only* for cleaning and then, only with cotton swabs and lightly…very lightly. And even that can't be done for the first three weeks it's on. She'll obviously need to have a catheter for an undetermined period. Her internal organs have really been rearranged drastically, and it's going to ease her comfort. She's going to be in a lot of pain…a *lot* of pain. She's probably going to want to be comforted, but be very, very careful about handling her for the first three to four weeks. When you see her, it's going to look far worse than it is. She has one drain tube coming out of her chest and another out of her stomach. Those will be in place for about three or four days, just to make sure she's not bleeding internally. We'll be able to see any blood collected in the serum, and it will tell us if we need to go back in. And she's badly bruised. Our biggest two enemies now are time and infection. Dr. Lyle and I have decided not to upgrade her condition yet. We'll re-evaluate that in twenty-four hours. Any questions for me?"

We looked at each other, back at Dr. Chen, and then all said, "No," at pretty much the same time. Dr. Chen disappeared, and we sat back down.

"Oh, shit! I need to call my office! They're probably panicking about now, wondering where I am," I exclaimed.

"I've already done that," grinned Pops.

"Thanks, Pops. You're the greatest. I mean it, you really are. Even though my family and I have pretty much made up over my being a lesbian, we're still not very close. I think of you and Martha as my real parents now. You know what they say, 'Blood is thicker than water, but love is thicker than blood.'"

"That's very sweet of you to say, Bells. You must know we think of you the same way."

"I do. Don't you have to get to work yourself?"

"Are you kidding me? I have over eight hundred hours of vacation and sick leave. I'm grandfathered under the old system, so they can't limit me. And I bet I have another six hundred hours of comp time. I could probably take off for six months, and there's nothing they can do about it. Besides, I don't want to take a taxi to work, and you and Martha would need the car."

"Can't you politely ask the Minneapolis police to give you a ride?"

"I could. I choose not to. Unless you're trying to get rid of me?"

"God, no. You know, hospital food is notoriously bad, but the breakfast isn't usually as bad as the rest of the day. I mean, how badly can eggs and bacon get ruined? Anybody else want to eat?" I asked.

We found our way to the cafeteria. My statement wasn't altogether correct. The bacon was a wee bit greasy, and I'd been at a summer camp once that had eggs like that—bland. Adding salt and pepper after the fact isn't the same as putting some in the mix prior to cooking, but at least my stomach was full. It took about another three hours before we got our courtesy call from the hospital letting us know Kathleen's ICU room number and the fact that she was moved in.

"We should go to one of the information desks and find out where that is," I said.

"Piffle! Follow me. I've questioned enough perps and suspects here that I know this place inside and out. Also, I had a couple fellow officers that were hurt and came here," declared Pops.

Within a few minutes, we had traversed a half-dozen hallways and were in the ICU. Even after talking to Dr. Chen, I wasn't prepared in the least for what I saw. Kathleen looked like somebody you'd see on the evening news in a story about a car bombing in another country. I quietly moved to the right side of the bed. I pulled the release and lowered the side guard. I didn't want to move Kathleen at all, so I leaned down, and gently rubbed my cheek against the back of her hand. Her eyes fluttered open a couple of times. I jumped back.

"Oh, Kathleen. I'm so sorry. I know you're hurt, but I just had to touch you, to feel you."

She moved her fingertips against the bed.

"You want me to do that again?" I queried.

Even though she had on a hard plastic cervical collar as a temporary precaution, she nodded. It was barely perceptible. I moved back down and just laid my face on her hand lightly. I stayed still, but Kathleen moved her fingers against my cheek. While I was there, I made yet one more promise to God, if only I could get Kathleen back. And not like she was before the crash, my perfect goddess. I didn't care about that. I just wanted her back with me. I fought too long and hard through life not to have her by my side forever. That was our promise—till death do us part—and I wasn't going to let death win this battle, not if I had my way.

We were in the room almost four hours when I finally got up and moved closer to the bed.

"Kathleen? Can you hear me?"

She made no motion. I'm sure the morphine was well and truly working its powers on her at that moment.

"We're going to go home now and try to get some sleep, but I'll be back tomorrow. I love you, baby. More than you could ever know. You have to pull through this. No matter how hard, no matter how long, always remember I'm here with you to help you every step of the way."

I touched my fingers to her hand, but she was completely asleep. I panicked for the slightest of seconds, then looked at the heart monitor and saw that everything was working.

When Pops and Martha dropped me off, I didn't want to be alone, but I also didn't want to impose any more than I had, and I knew that they would have done anything for me. So, I just went inside and draped myself across the couch. Within minutes, Tinkerbelle and Ivan came up to rub against me. I scratched them both until I finally fell asleep. When I woke up it was dark, and Ivan was sitting on my chest, licking his chops, and meowing.

"Go away. I'll feed you in a minute, pushy," I said, nudging him off onto the floor.

I'd been alone at night many, many times since marrying Kathleen: when she was on shift at the fire department, when she was in ambulances, when she was flying. But barring catastrophe, she would always come back in the morning. Then it struck me...barring catastrophe...that's what this was. And the danger level of flying helicopters at night was higher than riding in trucks on the ground, even if somebody did have to face the fire itself. Her new job was more impressive. It was to most people...but not me. I'd support whatever she wanted, but as sharp as she looked in her trooper's flight suit, I liked her St. Paul Fire Department uniform better. And I was never prouder of her, doing one of the most difficult jobs in the world, being a woman, and doing it as well as any man.

I forced myself up off the couch to feed Tinkerbelle and Ivan. While they were eating I was scratching the fur on their backs, talking to them like a crazy 'cat lady.'

"Well, Stinks, Ivan. Looks like it will be just the three of us here for a few weeks, at least. Your other mommy has gone and gotten herself all banged up."

I lost it right there. One second, I was fine. The next, all I could think about was losing Kathleen—about how I still might lose her, about how close I'd come to losing her, about how close they'd come to losing her in the OR—just everything. I couldn't live without Kathleen. Well, literally, I suppose I could, but I'd be one miserable soul, and I doubt I would ever recover from it. All joy would go out of my life. I got down on the floor, on my knees, and put my arms around the cats. They were a little annoyed because they were trying to eat, and they kept pulling away, but they didn't put up much of a real fight. And I didn't let go. I couldn't just yet. They were my medicine cats right now, the only things keeping me sane.

I finally let go of them and walked up the stairs to our bedroom. I opened the top drawer of my dresser and pulled out the manila folders. Most of the contents were photos of Kathleen working fires that were taken by a local newspaper photographer. There were also a couple newspaper articles. One was an award she got after she got her paramedic certification but before she transferred to Medic 4, an ambulance at Station 4. She'd done her practicum there early in the spring after we met and later was transferred there permanently. The award was given to Kathleen, one of only two people that won Firefighter of the Year. There were also a couple of photos of her during her training with Medic 4 and two or three of her in her St. Paul Fire and Rescue Paramedics' uniform. Same colors and patches as her firefighter days, but now in a jump suit with loops and bush pockets for medical tape, scissors, nylon straps, and a dozen other small items. I went through the entire stack, probably two hundred fifty in all. I was so proud of my baby. To me, she was just as perfect as I could have ever hoped for. I loved her looks, her character, her intelligence, and her kind heart...just everything about her. I'd never find another Kathleen. Never.

I rolled over on the bed, wrapped my arms around a pillow, and closed my eyes. When I woke up, it was dark, and I hadn't turned on any lights. I looked at the clock. It was right at two o'clock. Almost twenty-four hours later. How life can change in the blink of an eye. I went to the kitchen to make a salad. Instead, I ended up making a beef cotto salami sandwich on whole grain wheat bread using Green Goddess dressing instead of mayo or mustard, two slices of tomato, and a couple pieces of red leaf lettuce. Kathleen's favorite, and now mine.

I had to start thinking about things. It was obvious that Kathleen was going to take a long time to heal. I'd go to the hospital tomorrow, but starting on Thursday, I would have to get back to work. After she got out of the hospital, she was going to be at home for quite a while before she could do much of anything. It was also possible that she'd be on short-term disability for up to a year or so, then maybe permanent disability depending on how well and how fast she recovered. I'd obviously have to use all my available vacation time taking care of things and probably some family medical leave. I wouldn't get paid for that, of course, but I could borrow enough money to cover that. Plus, since our house payments were low, we'd been putting back quite a bit of money and had that for just such an emergency. Then, my mind went blank. I couldn't remember what I was even thinking about. It was too much to take in. I do remember thinking about being lucky, though, luckier than other people who had lost loved ones. I mentally vowed that I would honor my promises I'd made and would not forget them. When I was getting up from the table to go back to bed, I got the living shit scared out of me. There was someone in the living room…just sitting in my easy chair. I yelled out in fright, and the figure sitting in the dark talked back to me.

"Oh, I'm sorry, Bells. I came over and you didn't answer, so I let myself in. I checked on you upstairs, but you were hard asleep. I decided to leave you alone and just came down here to get comfortable."

"Pops! You almost gave me a heart attack! How long have you been here, anyway?"

"Oh, since maybe ten thirty or so."

"Go lie down in the guest bedroom on the bed at least. Can I get you something to eat?"

"No, I already raided the fridge when I got here. I'm good."

"Well, go upstairs and lie down. Don't sit there."

"Okay, I will. 'Night, kiddo."

"Night-night, Pops," I said, giving him a hug.

Jesus. I'd just been Friday the 13[th]ed. I was still edgy from being scared, and I wondered if I'd be able to get to sleep. After I put all the photos back up, I stretched out on the bed. I don't even remember closing my eyes.

❀ ❀ ❀

Ivan was under the covers, and Tinkerbelle was on top. They were playing a game of sheet hockey, which was their favorite way of waking me up before the alarm went off. Except today there was no alarm, so it was after their normal time, and I was sure they were bored and waiting for their breakfast. I yawned, stretched, and crawled out of bed myself. I looked in the guest bedroom, but Pops wasn't there, and the bed was made. I was beginning to wonder if I'd dreamed him up when I heard a pan clanking on the stove downstairs. Shortly after that, the smell of coffee made its way up to the bedroom. I got dressed, brushed my teeth, threw on a little sporty makeup, and bounded down the stairs.

"Hey, kiddo. You and I are going to eat a couple of pancakes, and we'll get a couple of fresh apple fritters and take them to Martha. She loves those things, and she can pop them in the microwave to warm them up. If we were at my house we'd have blueberry syrup, but we can either have syrup, black current jam, or lingonberry jam. Crazy Swedes!"

"Aren't you half Irish, half Swedish, Pops?"

"Yup, and that's why I'm having lingonberries."

"I keep feeling like we're going back to the hospital and she'll be sitting up drinking juice through a straw, and then in a couple of days, she'll be back home. She's really in for it, isn't she?"

"I'm not going to blow sunshine up your patootie, Bella. She's in a bad way. I've seen people in better shape, with fewer problems, die. Are you strong enough for that?"

"Please don't ask me that. You know I'm not. I don't know if I'm strong enough to go back to the hospital. It's the fact that I'll get Kathleen to move her fingertips twice and then lay there asleep for eight or nine hours, which is what she truly needs. I'll feel guilty that I want her awake more, and I'll be annoyed that she'll be all morphined up. All I want to do is sigh, huge sighs, over and over and over, like a stupid twit."

"Oh, I don't know. I don't think you'll be acting any differently than I will, or at least different than I'll be feeling."

"You say that, Pops, but you're always so strong. You always have been."

"I'm a throwback in some ways from a day when you were expected to keep on with things. I mean, sure, I have feelings, but it's always one foot in front of the other."

We ate in silence after that. What would have been delightful any other day was a meal I hardly took notice of. Twice, I started to get up with my plate, and twice, Pops grabbed my plate, stabbed the air above it, and cleared his throat to get me to finish. Finally, I'd managed to nearly clean my plate, and he didn't fight me. I got up and washed the dishes and scratched the cats for a minute. I didn't have the words to explain to them what had happened to their other mommy...how she was hurt...how she might not live. They were words I couldn't even admit to myself. Not yet. Pops grabbed a small plastic plate and fork to make a proper go for Martha to eat her fritter, and away we went for the day.

We stopped at a small donut shop that was just a family affair but was clogged with morning business men and women. It seemed to take forever for Pops to return to his truck, and all I could think about was getting to the hospital. The idea crossed my mind, though, that the idea was ludicrous. I'd get there, and Kathleen would be so heavily sedated she wouldn't even know I was there. Was I a terrible person to want her not to be sedated just long enough to know I was there for her? God, I must be a total, stone-cold bitch.

The traffic was a nightmare, or as we say in the twin cities, normal. We would have been better off waiting an hour for the traffic to die off, but we were not just supporting Kathleen, we were supporting Martha as well. Finally, we were in the parking ramp for the hospital, and I breathed my first big sigh of the day. At least I was going to be near my Kathleen. Win, lose, or draw in this fight, I was going to be at arms' distance again.

❋ ❋ ❋

"Hey, sleepy head. We thought you might want some breakfast, so we brought you a couple of fresh apple fritters. We just microwaved them down the hall and got you some fresh coffee."

Martha looked right through me as though I wasn't there for a few seconds before finally focusing.

"Well, I always said that I never got the long, sleepless nights being a mother. Even before Kathleen opened up to me, especially in her teens, I had a slew of long, sleepless nights. Nothing like this, though. Not even close."

Pops set the coffee down in front of Martha on the shelf made by the window, and I set out the plate with the fritters along with the fork from home.

"Mmm. Boy, these are so much better than yesterday's breakfast. That, my friends, was ghastly!"

"Well, take your time, but when you're ready, I'll take you home to shower and get some good sleep in our bed," Pops threw in.

"Oh, I slept quite well…fifteen or twenty minutes at a time, but the shower I'd gladly use."

"Did Kathleen wake up at all during the night?" I asked.

"You might as well know because you're going to find out. About three-fifteen or so she got to the point where the pain meds weren't able to maintain, so she went into about an hour and a half of fitful, restless behavior. Oh, honey, she was in the most God-awful pain, I'm afraid."

I looked up suddenly and saw two people approaching us.

"Mama! Daddy! What are you doing here?" I practically screamed, jumping up and running to them, hugging them both simultaneously.

"Well, our daughter-in-law is hurt in the most awful way, and it's what you do," answered Dad.

"We were just so concerned," answered Mama.

"I'm so glad you're here."

"We have to leave the day after tomorrow because there are a couple of planning and board meetings that I just can't duck, but we thought it's the least we could do for you," said my dad.

"Hi, Steven. Hi, Della," said Pops, extending his hand.

"Hello, Kevin. Hello, Martha," they both chimed.

They both sat down while Martha devoured her fritter. We had gotten her two, so she could have one after lunch, but after she had eaten the first one, she went to the microwave and re-warmed the second one. Pops wasn't kidding, she loved them.

I pulled a chair up to the side of the bed and pulled Kathleen's hand across mine, laying her fingers across my fingertips.

"Kathleen, baby, it's me. I don't know if you can tell I'm here right now, but I'm here as much as I can be. I'm here about half the day for a while until I have to go back to work. Well, it looks like you really went and screwed this one up big time. Just had to play big shot one too many times, didn't you, my sexy thing?" I whispered to her, my voice barely audible as I leaned down over the bed.

I started singing a song we'd both loved that played on the radio a couple of months after we got married. It was Christina Perri's "A Thousand Years".

I was both startled and surprised when her fingers curled over mine twice in response. I tried talking to her beyond that but got nothing in return. I stopped talking to her after about twenty minutes, but I didn't pull my hand back.

"If it's all right with you, Bella, I'm going to have Kevin run me home, so I can turn back into a human again. Maybe a shower and a nap in my own bed for a change. Will you be okay? Anything I can bring you?"

"No, go ahead, Martha. We'll be fine. It's just us girls sitting here talking amongst ourselves."

I thought I could feel Kathleen curling her fingers at that, but it might well have been wishful thinking. Pops and Martha had been gone about forty-five minutes. I was at the side of the bed just to the left of Kathleen with the side bar down, so I could hold her hand on top of mine. Suddenly, I had the funniest thought.

"Baby, when you go back by Station 7 for a visit, you'll be able to strip down to your underwear and show those pansies what a real scar looks like, don'tcha know?" I chortled.

"Oh, sweetie, don't make me laugh."

"Kathleen? Kathleen? Are you awake? Baby?"

But that's all that I got out of her. One line. And she didn't even move her hand. But at least I'd gotten a couple of small replies out of her, and it was still early in the day. I gathered up a couple pillows and made a little nest out of them, getting comfortable on my side of Kathleen's bed, settling in for the day. Mama and Daddy finally headed out to find a good restaurant and then return to their hotel room for the day, settling in for one very long, very uneventful day.

I snuggled up next to Kathleen's hand, rubbing my lips across her fingertips as lightly as a breeze, and began to sing our song once again:
"Hearts beet fast
Colors and promises
How to brave...."

I must have sung the entire song three times, and my voice began to quaver, tears streaming down my cheeks freely, my hands gripping the edge of the sheet in my fists, terrified that I was losing her. Part of me wanted my determination alone to bring Kathleen back to health, part of me was just a scared little girl, cringing in the dark, all alone. Why couldn't this be a business problem I could just resolve?

Martha and Pops came back in the early afternoon, and the three of us were lazily snoozing in the room for the rest of the day...until about half past seven in the evening, that is. That's when all the instruments hooked up to Kathleen simultaneously erupted, or so it seemed. I barely had time to stand up and scream for a nurse when there were three of them in the room. The first one in commanded us to leave the room, which we did quickly. It took about fifteen or twenty minutes to get everything settled down, but of course it seemed like an eternity.

"We have Kathleen sedated, but this time, not so much morphine. We need her a bit more responsive to the surgeon. She'll be down in about an hour or so if all goes as planned. This is not uncommon, so don't look at this as either a bad event or a good event. It's just something that's happened, okay?" the main nurse passed on to us just before disappearing down the hallway.

"Well, if she's going into surgery again that means I'm staying. Why don't the two of you go home?" I asked Pops and Martha.

"Nonsense. I wouldn't think of it," said Martha before even thinking.

She truly was Kathleen's mother. Just then, there was a bustle of noise in the ICU and a chorus of "Keep your voices down!" and other comments to that effect.

Mike, Oliver—a huge man whose name was Ambrocio (he was ethnically Greek, earning him the nickname Greek)—and Brian, all fire fighters in St. Paul with Kathleen at Station 7 when she was still a firefighter before moving to Medic 4, came stumbling in like a bunch of pub-crawling drunkards.

"What's this crap about a paid vacation, Pope? Slacker detail is over!" Greek was first to shout out, way too loud for the ICU.

"Look, guys. It must be spa day. Kathleen's got her eyes covered and pillows under her knees. Can you believe this? Too pampered and special to ride a truck or a bus anymore, only wants to ride whirly-gigs with jets in 'em. Well, ain't she highbrow?" chimed in Brian.

"You know, you guys make me wonder why I ever called you my friends," Kathleen managed to croak out.

"Oh, Kathleen!" I shrieked as I jumped up and grabbed her hand, not caring whether I was hurting her at that exact moment in time.

"Shut the fuck up. My head hurts like Tito Puente is playing the marimbas inside it. No kidding. And I'm sooo thirsty. Get a nurse to bring me some water," she fairly commanded.

I picked up the call button and started pushing it over and over and over, trying to get a nurse there as quickly as possible, as if hitting it more than once made a difference. I needn't have bothered.

"Gentlemen, I appreciate your enthusiasm, but if you can't quiet down I'm going to run the lot of you out of here."

The four firefighters all pulled out their IDs with badges. The nurse picked up her nametag with the letters RN, CNP following her name.

"Oh, hell yeah, we can all play some of that game if you want. And if y'all want, we can go snatch up my purse and I'll show you that I'm 4/4-degree Lakota, Sisseton tribe. Wanna throw down with that? Now, either be quiet or get *out*!"

"Okay, we'll be quiet, but she's talking, and she wants some water. That's good, right?" asked Greek.

"She say that, or are you making this up as you go?" the nurse asked.

"No, it's actually me. I'm dry. I need some hydration," Kathleen managed.

"Well, Ms. Pope. Let me tell you a little bit about what's going on around you. You're getting about one liter every three hours, so you don't need any hydration. Your catheter is draining nice and steady, a good output. You gave everybody quite a fright, you know."

"How's my potassium, my WBC, and my RBC?" asked Kathleen.

"Let me get your chart," said the nurse as she left to go to the nurses' station.

"What's with all this talking shop? This is a genuine time off from the job. Kick it and shut it, Kaths," piped in Oliver.

"And I expect every one of you to do anything that Bella needs, no questions asked. There's plenty of you between the three shifts, so you can all throw in together."

"Oh, yeah. That goes without saying," they all chimed in together.

"Kathleen, it's not like I'm an invalid. I'm a twenty-seven-year-old woman in the prime of her life. There's nothing I can't handle."

"I know that, but now that you're pregnant...."

The hoops and the hollers went through the roof! We'd not told anybody yet that I was pregnant, and as Nurse Grey Eyes (that was actually her name) came back into the room, her glare preceded her.

"I. Told. You! Now, you need to leave. All of you!" she said, pointing to the door.

On the way out, they continued to make noise, congratulating me, telling me they'd call, and telling Kathleen they'd be back soon.

"Okay, here we are. Let's see...Sodium is 137, which is expected since we're running fluids through you like nobody's business. Potassium is 4.5, a little on the low side, but again, you're being flushed, so still, a good number...."

"What about protein?" asked Kathleen.

"12.6. And before you ask, your WBC is about three thousand, an astonishingly low count considering you're battling infections. RBC is about 4.0, but that's because you'd been bleeding badly, and you're having to catch up. Not too bad for somebody with a ten percent chance of living. I'm told the only thing that got you here is your supreme physique," ventured the nurse.

"Hey, that's my wife you're talking about! Don't you go peeking at her physique!" I laughed.

Nurse Grey Eyes smiled at that one. I hadn't moved or said anything until that point. I was still holding Kathleen's hand and sitting on the side of the bed.

"Okay, so why is she feeling so dehydrated?" I finally asked, breaking the momentary silence.

"Oh, that? That's just a major case of chapped lips. She's breathing with gauze over her face, which traps moisture, and against her skin it works as a wick to draw the moisture out of her skin. I've got just the thing for that though. Normally we'd go with ice chips, but we don't want any movement of the face bones yet, so I'll bring you a juice box, and you can use the straw to drip water through her lips. Try not to get much outside her lips or it will aggravate the chapped area. Meanwhile I'll let the doctor know and we'll get some ointment ordered. And if you want, you can squeeze the juice from the box for yourself. Just no juice for her. We have to monitor her total fluid intake from all sources, and for now, it's all through IVs. I'll go get that for you now. Oh, and congratulations, Mom."

"Oh, thank you. I'm still getting used to it myself."

FURTHER INTO FIRE

Suddenly from the hallway, Pops and Martha came wandering back into Kathleen's room.

"Look who decided to open her black and blue eyes and talk to us for a little while. I'm glad you came back while she was still awake."

"So, it's true then, Kitten?"

"What's that, Pops?"

"You two been shopping on the internet?"

"What?"

"You got Bells knocked up, sure's Mrs. Gustaffsen's got apple pies?"

"Pops!"

"Kevin!" yelled Martha.

"Well, am I or am I not going to be a grandpa? I know we had you when we were pretty old, but you know I'd pretty much figured that all and all, you know, with how things were, that grandkids were off the table for me. I mean I was okay with that and all...."

"Pops, do me a favor. Shut up. Stop being a man, and shut up," Kathleen declared.

"Indeed, Kevin Pope. A little decorum would go a long way!" spoke up Martha.

Pops reached one hand out to me, took my seemingly tiny hand into his big bear paw, and rubbed his eyes with his other. Martha wrapped her arms around him, and we all stood together, intertwined there in a moment that seemed like forever. And that is how we came to tell Martha and Pops that they were going to be 'grands.' And that is when I finally started believing I wasn't going to lose my beloved wife Kathleen.

❦ ❦ ❦

"Good morning, Sunshine! Are you awake yet?" I asked cheerfully, walking into the ICU.

Kathleen's eyes fluttered a bit before opening. I had no idea whether she grimaced or smiled or something in between underneath the gauze bandages she wore as a mask below the plastic plate on her face, which was holding everything perfectly still.

"I'd give fifty cents for a cup of coffee, a dollar for a bottle of water, and a full five bucks for a salami sandwich."

"I bet you would, little girl."

"The doctor is supposed to come by today and talk to me about my recovery process and all that...maybe make a schedule."

"Kathleen, for once in your life why don't you relax? You'll get there. You've been in here three weeks, and already you think you should be flying tomorrow. Get over it. If it's any consolation, my admin is furious at you for crashing your helicopter. It's totally upset our routine."

"Tell Courtney that Norman didn't exactly plan on killing himself and maiming everybody else that morning," Kathleen managed.

It was the first of many things that were to follow. Maybe not meant to be hurtful, but still, who knows from what terrible depths it came.

"Oh, honey. I'm sure that's not what she meant. I'm so sorry. To tell you the truth, I'm not even sure she knows that Norman died in the accident. You know, it's all just so routine, and we never think about things going really wrong."

"Yeah, well, this time, they did. They went way wrong. No high winds, no smoke, no icing, nothing. We took off, we caught a wire, we flipped over, and we came down. Hard. End of fucking story."

"Kathleen! Stop it! You're scaring me!" I yelled out to her.

"You should go to work today and get caught up."

"Kathleen, what in the world has gotten into you? What have I done to deserve this?" I demanded

"Deserve what? I'm just saying you've been babysitting me for weeks and not working. Courtney's right. You should at least go in for a while and keep your head in the game."

"Look, if you don't want me to be here, tell–"

"For today, I don't want you to be here, Bella. Okay? Just…Augh!"

I gathered up my purse and jacket, and I stormed out, crying. It was the first time in over three years I'd left Kathleen without saying goodbye, without kissing her, without acknowledging her. It clawed at me from inside like nothing I'd felt in my nearly thirty years. It was almost as bad as the day the patrolman came to our house to notify me of Kathleen's accident. Why? Why did she lash out at me? What could I have done? That moment began the first of what was to become thousands of little moments of self-doubt and questioning for which I had no answer. Kathleen and I were the dynamic duo, right? Less than a week after meeting her, she basically said not just half of what is mine is yours, but all of what is mine is yours. I just didn't get it. I banged into people randomly throughout the hallways and into the parking garage where I got into my car and drove home through a wall of tears. At the last second before going home, I turned left and drove to Pops' and Martha's house. I hoped they were home. Gladly, they were. I steeled myself in front of the door, then knocked, daubing my eyes one last time with a tissue.

"Well, Martha. Look who it is. Come on inside and let us fire up the coffee maker," said Pops as he grabbed me by the elbow and pulled lightly at me.

"Hi, Pops."

I couldn't take another step. I fell into him and started crying full gale.

"There, there. The worst of it's over now...we're pretty sure. Assuming she can sidestep any major infections, she should do a pretty good job at recovery. These things have a way of working themselves out."

"Pops, she threw me out. She said she didn't want me there. That's truly the first cross thing she's said since we've met. I mean, we've had little squabbles, but we've never really had an honest argument before today," I managed to get out through a nose full of snot, eyes full of tears, and hiccups.

"Come on in here. Let's get some coffee going and talk."

"Maybe some chocolate milk? The baby?"

"Oh, for Pete's sakes! Yeah, you betcha!"

Martha came in from the utility room and upon seeing me pretty much gathered I wasn't in good condition. She gave me a hug and patted the back of my head but said nothing. Pops got out three huge mugs. I guess the talk was going to be a long one, which was fine for me. I wasn't sure what I needed, but I needed something. He made coffee for the two of them and hot cocoa for me.

"There's something that's not talked about a lot. Hypertension is pretty common among firefighters and policemen. Lots of other professions too, just prevalent in ours. And after surviving heart attacks or bypasses following attacks of angina, there's a lot of weird mental shit that goes on. The studies are predominately of men, and the window is usually longer term than the month that Kathleen's been banged up, but essentially, Kathleen died many times over. Waiting, on the trip in, in the O.R., and that does something to your mind. I'd like to tell you it always clears up. I know one sergeant that sold everything, gave his wife all but twenty thousand dollars, and moved to Alaska. Is it rare? Absolutely. But she's always been the one in control of everyone's destiny...even when she met you. Now, she's not in control. She's been in control since she's been twelve, this is new territory. For now, I'd say, 'Just give her time.'"

"This is not how I planned this going. We were, by the way, going to tell you after getting the pictures tomorrow. So, Martha, wanna go get some baby pictures tomorrow? First snaps of the spawn?"

"Ultrasound? I'd love to go! I couldn't ever have kids, so Harold and I never had things like that. You know, I heard not so very long ago that both the kids he had with that hussy he hooked up with after he dumped me to the curb got busted in a meth lab thing up north somewhere. Makes you proud to be a parent, doesn't it?" Martha veritably cackled.

"You know, it's so seldom you have an evil thought. It comes out with such…such…."

"Yeah, doesn't it though! What time do we go?"

"It's at ten o'clock at the Clarkston Clinic. I'll come by here and pick you up."

"Then, if you two are going to do that, I'm going to go to work tomorrow and arrest a few reams of paper. It's the least I could do for the good of society."

"Oh, the very least, Pops! Thanks. I really needed to come over here. I didn't know what else to do," I said.

"My only concern is that you gave it any thought at all. Next time, just come by. Or call. Or whatever."

"Okay, Pops. I promise. Mmm…" I said as I gave him the hugest of hugs.

"I'll see you tomorrow morning about nine, then, dear," Martha said.

"Okay, bye-bye," I said and drove off.

I was better, but I certainly wasn't great. Hell, I wasn't even good. And it was way too early in the day to be able to say I'd gotten through it. I decided to go all in and get junk food. After I got home, I picked up the phone and called Courtney.

"Hey. How's Kathleen?"

"Not a topic of discussion. Unless you've got solid plans for the evening, I need you to come with me to starch your knickers from the inside out and eat fried food with me. Come to the pub and get some fried walleye and mushrooms. And of course, grab a cab, so we can drink…heavily. Can do?"

"Wait one. Hey, Craig? You got anything going tonight? Even better. Craig is going to drive me and pick me up to save some money. Henricksen's, I assume, since we're frying everything?"

"You got it. See you at six thirty."

"Be there or be square!"

"And Courtney? Thanks. I really need this."

"Pish-posh. See you in about two hours," she clicked off.

Ivan was about fourteen, and Tinkerbelle was seventeen. I'd already decided that I was going to surprise Kathleen with a new pair of littermates to get younger kittens in the house, but now that I was doubting myself, I wasn't so sure, which was stupid, I realized. Of course, I was still doubting myself even though I'd made an appointment two weeks ago to go see a litter and pick out two kittens this coming weekend. I was already feeling less upset, but I still had a ways to go on that one, and I had already determined there was going to be lots of food involved. If only I could drink! My phone rang. It was my mother. Not until tomorrow. I didn't want to have this conversation this afternoon. She still couldn't let go of all the drama. I decided to take a shower and dress up for a change. I hadn't in quite a while. At six o'clock, I grabbed my purse and made for the front door. Traffic was heavy for a Wednesday evening, but I still got there before Courtney.

"Oh, sorry I'm late. My boss is a bit of a bitch, and since she's been out the last few weeks I've been burning the candle at both ends trying to do tons of stuff I don't normally have to do. Seriously, Craig forgot he was playing my chauffeur for the night. He'd lose his head if it weren't screwed on!"

"I met your boss once. She's an angel. You should tell her."

"She's a third my age. I wouldn't think of it."

"Oh, maybe because you're older you want her job?" I laughed.

"Not at gunpoint!" Courtney cackled back, holding her hand up in the air to get our waiter.

"What can I bring you ladies tonight?" he asked.

"Two dark draughts. Twenty ouncers."

"No, I think I'll just have an iced tea with orange slices, please," I said.

"No, you'll have dark beer. Bring her dark beer."

"Seriously. My head hurts a little. And with everything going on with Kathleen and in my life, I just need not to drink right now," I smiled up at the waiter, who nodded and disappeared with our order.

"Are you pregnant?"

"What? Did you start early at home?"

"You're in a mood, you're Lil' Miss Houston, and you don't want a beer. Are you pregnant, yes or no?"

I couldn't answer. I just stared at her, my eyes tearing up, the tears streaming down my cheeks, saying nothing, not moving, and not doing anything.

"Ahhh! I guessed it! Am I good or what?" Courtney said pounding the air with her fists and stomping her feet.

"So, I went to the hospital this afternoon. Kathleen kicked me out of her room in the ICU. Out. Told me to leave. Can you imagine how that made me feel? It was the cruelest thing I've ever seen one human do to another. Doesn't she know how that made me feel?"

"Honey, you have to understand. She's been in a five-star rodeo, and she's just been thrown off the biggest bronc there is. Of course, there will be problems inside her. A person can't go through that and not have problems, no matter how strong they are. But I've been around Kathleen for three years now, and I'm a pretty good judge of character. This will work itself out. I promise you. So, for tonight, let's not even talk about the bad things anymore. Okay? Good. How far along are you? This is so cool!" Courtney practically shrieked.

"Well, tomorrow morning is my first ultrasound. It's supposed to be twelve weeks, give or take. Not really sure, of course, but close to it, in any case."

"You never show it, but do you barf your toes up in the mornings?" Courtney cackled.

I'm not sure why she was in a cackling mood, a cackling and drinking beer mood. The beer seemed to be flowing quickly.

"I get the feeling I'm about to take on a job where everybody thinks I'm supposed to be this new super mom type that wants to love and cuddle every baby out there. Queasy but not tossing my cookies. Truthfully? I want my own baby. I don't want to be shown a picture of your ugly baby and told it's the most beautiful thing in the world. All I'm looking to get out of this is a healthy baby boy or baby girl…no more, no less. Does that make me a bad person?"

"No, I get you. The next thing they'll start throwing at you is all the commercial stuff. Cribs, changing tables, carriers, clothes, blankets, toys, and other crap! Then, they'll all want to touch you. Invasive bastards!" Courtney laughed.

"Now, comes the fun part," I said.

"Oh, yeah?" asked Courtney.

"How to tell my mother. So, you know about the day that she just showed up at my wedding and finally admitted that it was okay that I was gay, right?" I asked.

"Uh-huh."

"Well, this is a subject that has not been brought up…not even once. I don't think she knows it's even in the realm of possibility that lesbians can have children. In her mind's eye she probably thinks that we're sterile, among other things." I just had to laugh.

"Got somebody to go with you tomorrow? I'd be happy to go with you if you need me."

"I've got Martha going with me, so that's covered. But I do appreciate the offer. I really do. Oh, life is just so crazy right now. I do get everything that is going on, but it doesn't stop it from seeming like it's all just a little bit crazy. A little bit too crazy, if you know what I mean?" I sighed.

Luckily, the waiter brought our food, and we were able to just take it in for a moment, redirecting our madness of the moment although Courtney still managed to tell me what harebrained things people back at the office were managing to spring on each other every day unwittingly. For the first time since arriving in Minnesota, I honestly didn't miss the office whatsoever. I felt like the things that were before me were far greater in scope, and life was so much more precious and meaningful than all the myriad of things that made up my day-to-day life in the corporate world. Trite, yes. But life sometimes is just too precious....

When I finally got home, it was almost ten thirty. My parents don't usually like getting calls that late. They like to go to bed and watch television, so they're not usually asleep yet, but late calls bother them sometimes.

"Bella? Is something wrong? Is Kathleen okay?" answered Mom.

"Yes, yes. Everything is okay. It's not that. Is Daddy in town tonight? Is he there with you?"

"Yes, we're in bed now, as usual. What is it, dear?"

I took in a large breath of air and let out a huge sigh.

Mama handed the phone to Dad.

"Doodles? What's going on? How's Kathleen?" asked Dad.

"She's doing better. Gaining more strength."

"What's wrong?"

"Nothing. Why?"

"Don't bullshit me. I can hear it in your voice. Something's wrong. Has there been a setback?" he asked starting to sound very concerned.

I started to stream tears, holding back the sobs that I knew were seconds away.

"What is it? Tell me. What is it?"

"Daddy, she's shutting me out. She doesn't want me there," I said as I let go for real.

"Trust me, Doodles. Tragic illnesses often bring on strange reactions. A lot of times it's just a matter of the person thinking that they've been disfigured, and they don't want anybody to see them, or they're crippled, and they don't want to be a burden to anybody. Just give it time. Don't worry, she'll come around. I'll talk to you soon, okay?"

"Bella? You know you can call me more often, don't you? Just to talk or whatever?" Mom asked when she got the phone back.

"I know. Well, it's late, so I'll let you two get back to your television. Night," I said hanging up, not even waiting for a response.

I cried all the way from then until I was in bed, under the covers, and sound asleep. The next morning, when I put on makeup, I only put on blush and eyeshadow, so it wouldn't run. I was prepared for more crying, although I managed not to. Martha saw to that.

❄ ❄ ❄

"Martha, if it's okay with you I'd rather go back to the house first, instead of to the hospital. I think I'd rather deal with my mother before Kathleen, if you don't mind."

"Oh, I don't mind at all," she said

Once we got settled at the house with fresh coffee, I prepared to scan an image and send it to my parents.

"Which one of these do you think will be a better picture?" I asked, holding up three or four of the ultrasound images.

"I think that one right there," she said, pointing to one.

"Well, no guts no glory. There she goes."

And with that, I scanned the image and sent it attached to an email with no text; I just sent the image. Martha and I sat and chatted, sipping coffee, and waiting. It wasn't long before the emails started coming back to me. The first one was from my mother wanting to know, 'What in the world that was all about?' Instead of emailing her this time, I picked up my phone and dialed her number.

"What in the Wide, Wide World of Sports did you just send me?" she asked.

"I would've thought after all the years of Daddy being in the medical field you would know what an ultrasound is," I said rather matter-of-factly.

"Yes, I can see it's an ultrasound, but of what, or rather, of whom?" she asked rather exasperatedly.

"Your grandbaby, dingle fart."

I waited. I wanted it to sink in. Apparently, I had to wait longer than I originally thought. There was this enormous silence on the line.

"But I thought…I mean, you and Kathleen are…And she's in the hospital… Oh, Bella. For goodness sakes, this is just not funny! Please explain this to me. You're giving Mama a terrible headache!"

"Yes, Kathleen is in the hospital, but she's only been there three weeks. I'm twelve weeks pregnant. We used a donor. You didn't think Nancy and Bryce were the only two that could give you grandkids, did you?"

I looked over at Martha, who picked up a couch cushion and wrapped her arms around it, burying her face in it and trying to suppress her laughter. That only made it harder for me to keep from laughing, which was already a chore. I must admit, sometimes my mother couldn't buy a vowel.

"Belladonna, promise me this is not some twisted, sick, April fool's joke!" she said in the sternest of voices.

"No, Mama. It's for real. You're going to be a grandma again. Anyway, I have to go because that's Daddy trying to ring in. I'll talk to you later. Bye-bye."

"And your mother actually sells million-dollar homes?" Martha managed to ask between laughs.

"Oh, and she gets worse, believe me. It's because the people she sells to are even stupider. I mean, I guess she's not stupid, but at times, she has no sense about her at all. There's me and Daddy and Bryce, and then there's her and Nancy. That's the split in the family gene pool."

"Hello, Daddy? What's new?" I asked.

"Well, I would say from ten to thirteen weeks, and although I would need to see more to give you a better evaluation, I'm ecstatic! I'd say this is a little bit of good news to go along with the bad that we've had this last week with Kathleen being in the hospital and all. This should cheer her up some, shouldn't it?"

"Actually, I haven't shown her the pictures yet. I just had them taken this morning, and we haven't gone to the hospital yet. I'm not sure Kathleen will be up for them anyway. She's still pretty out of it," I ventured.

"Honey, trust me on this one. She'll be interested. Well, I have to run. Thank you for the email. It really brightened my otherwise dreary day here at the sausage grind. Love you."

"Love you too, Daddy. Bye."

I'd been fumbling with the pictures in my hand for about fifteen minutes while talking on the phone. The moment of reckoning was at hand. I got up and took the coffee cups into the kitchen, rinsed them out, and placed them in the sink. Then, I walked back into the living room, picked up my purse, the photos, and my keys, and held out my hand to wave Martha toward the car. Martha was usually very good about making small talk without making it seem like small talk, but today we rode in silence toward the hospital. We also parked in silence, rode the elevator in silence, and trod the hallways in silence. But nothing could prepare me for what I saw when I got to the ICU unit. There, sitting in the chair, was Melanie. She was holding Kathleen's hand in hers.

"Melanie, I think you need to leave now. You know we're married, and you know there is no good that can come out of you being here, so

I'm going to warn you now...if you come back, I'll have you arrested. Is that clear?" I asked very clearly and concisely.

"I'm sorry, I..." she said as she got up from her chair at the side of the bed and squeezed past Martha and me, quickly exiting the room.

"I thought I'd seen the last of that girl a long time ago. She broke Kathleen's heart," said Martha. "Well, I'll be back in just a minute. You go ahead and say hi to Kathleen. I'm going to step out here for just a second," she said as she put her purse down.

"So, Kathleen...Can you hear me right now?" I asked quietly.

"Yeah, I can hear you. Why are you standing over there?"

"I understand that things are really, really bad right now. But can you tell me why Melanie was here this morning?" I asked with emphasis.

"Do you remember Dalton Stevenson? Our air ambulance patient? Dalton is her uncle. He was here at HCMC too. He died this morning."

"Oh, my God! I feel like such a heel! I just got through telling her–" I cried out.

"I heard you. Don't worry about it. Trust me, she did go way too far, and I just played possum until she was out of the room, for both our sakes."

"If you're up to opening your eyes, I may have something that will change your mood just a little bit. Maybe. Just a teensy little bit," I proffered.

"Would you take the juice straw and dribble a few drops of water on my eyelids, so I can open them and focus."

I did, gladly, of course. Anything for my Kathleen.

"You know, if you're really not up to this we can do this later. I can even come back later, if you'd rather," I ventured timidly.

"Why would I rather that?" Kathleen riddled.

I placed droplets of water into her eyes, then dabbed at them with tissue paper to soak up the excess.

"Well, after yesterday...."

"Could we just forget about yesterday, please?"

"I brought something with me to show you. I wasn't sure, but I thought just maybe it would cheer you up a little bit. I've kind of been fighting inside my head whether I should show you these or not since it's something that's been given to us, and something else is being taken away from you, but in the long run, I hope you feel joy and not sadness when you see these..." and I slowly began to pull the images of the ultrasound out of the envelope.

One by one, I held them up so Kathleen could see them. On about the third one she reached out the fingertip on her right hand and raised it slightly toward the picture. I lowered the picture, so she could touch the surface with the fingertip of her forefinger.

"I'm not really sure. It's way too early to tell. This could just be a tailbone, or it could be part of Kevin Pope the II. To tell you the truth, I thought you'd probably rather have a little boy, so you could play firefighter, policeman, helicopter pilot...and all that other crap you do. Although, the picture of us in our dresses still staggers my imagination. You are gorgeous in a uniform to me, but seeing you dressed up as a woman will be my favorite. Our ball gowns."

Kathleen's fingers were scurrying, trying to move on to another picture, so I kept moving from picture to picture, showing her our little baby, alive inside me. *Our* baby.

"Can you imagine Kathleen? There won't be any other eighteen-month-old baby on the block who can drag a fifty-foot, three-quarter inch, red rubber hose *full of water* to full-length in twenty seconds. A true firefighter. And it won't matter whether it's a boy *or* a girl."

I put my first two fingers inside Kathleen's hand and she squeezed my fingers. At that point, I hoped that yesterday was just a hiccup. I certainly wanted no more days like that. Kathleen and I had a life together completely free of drama up until that point, but somehow, I had a foreshadowing that things had somehow changed, and it scared me because I didn't know how much things had changed.

"Our baby," she managed almost imperceptibly before her eyes completely closed.

My heart melted. Later tonight, things could change. The Santa Ana winds could start a firestorm, the monsoons of Western Thailand could wash away the hillsides, and volcanoes worldwide could blow their caps...but for now, this exact moment in time, all was right with the world, and all was right between Kathleen and me.

※ ※ ※

After taking a month off work to care for Kathleen in the hospital, I finally decided it was time to get my big girl panties on and go back into the office to start taking care of business again. It was surprising to find out how much I'd missed and how much had gotten done in my absence. All morning long, I had to fight the urge to keep go back home and turn one month into two, but that wasn't reasonable, and it wasn't good business.

There were flowers for me everywhere. They were on my desk, on filing cabinets, on extra chairs, and even a couple of ivy plants were sitting on the floor. The very first thing I did, was have Courtney gather up every last one and have them delivered to the nursing home where Kathleen read as a volunteer. I knew they would enjoy them much more than I would.

"Courtney, staff meeting in five minutes. Let the whole team know. Make sure nobody's stuck in the bathroom. I want everybody on board, and I do mean *everybody*," I shouted to her through the telephone.

"You betcha, boss," I heard as I saw her get up and start making the rounds, letting everybody know to get to the conference room.

I quickly pulled together the accounts I wanted to discuss in our meeting and put them in the stack on the corner of my desk along with a notebook. I quietly sat at my desk for a couple of minutes, rapping my fingernails on my notebook, then decided to go into the conference room early. There were only three people in the conference room when I got there, but more started filing in quickly. After our entire team was seated, I looked around the room, saying nothing for a couple of minutes, then I slowly and deliberately began to speak.

"I get it, I really do. And I understand that the feeling is genuine. I want everyone in the room to say one time all together, 'We're sorry about Kathleen.' What happened was regrettable, but it was an accident, no more no less, and in time we'll get through it. While I'd like to think that we here at Pfister-Blankenship are collectively as sympathetic as any humans can be, we do still have a business to run. I intend to see that we run it, and run it very well at that," I concluded.

I went on for the next hour and a half, going over our major projects, where we stood on each, and what we needed to do to prepare ourselves for each of them. I talked about where we were ahead and why we shouldn't give any slack in those areas, but in general I kept everything very upbeat. I turned this into a rally rather than just a ho-hum meeting. Gradually, everybody made their way back to their desk, and all that remained in the conference room was a few odd bits of paper, my stack of files, and the entire yellow pad that Courtney had just taken notes on with respect to our meeting.

"Well, you think they hate me?" I asked Courtney, picking up my stack of folders.

"I'll tell you this, there weren't any droopy eyes in that meeting! Everybody looked like they'd had a triple espresso with an energy drink chaser! Hah!" Courtney said.

"And you don't think I went too far with the 'Let's get it all out in the open once and for all' bit? After seeing all the flowers around, I just had these visions in my head of trying to tiptoe through shards of broken glass everywhere I walked, and that's just not my style."

"Oh, you don't have to convince me. Personally, I think this little bit of Bitchdom might be just the ticket to get everybody up on their toes without getting them too close to the train siding, if you know what I mean. Not so much to wind everybody up as to keep them up in a time of crisis without stressing them too much or carrying the weight yourself. I'd say another brilliant play, Madame! Hat's off all 'round!"

"Well, let's not go that far. But truthfully, even without this stuff with me and Kathleen, there are other things in the works with our group this quarter. I just want us to shine, no holds barred."

"I get you, I get you. So how did 'picture day' go with Kathleen?" Courtney asked.

"Pretty well. When I got there, her ex was there, sitting at the side of the bed holding Kathleen's hand. At first, it really bothered me. I told her if she ever came back, I'd have her arrested. But after she left, Kathleen told me that the guy they pulled out of the air ambulance was her uncle, and he died that morning. I don't know what to make of it, truthfully. Naturally, I don't like it," I concluded.

I managed to keep my mind on work for most of the day, then slipped home to feed the cats before making an evening of it at the hospital. After changing clothes and dropping some food in the cat bowls, I drove through a drive-in fast-food restaurant and spent five minutes in the parking lot scarfing down the cardboard food. I finally managed to get to the hospital on the tail end of the traffic for the evening. As I approached the ICU, that little hand was knotting itself up inside my stomach. There was a lot of noise coming from the ward. At first, I didn't hear Kathleen, but then, clear as a bell, there it was.

"Look, I told you the catheter hurt, so I took it out. I had no idea what was keeping you guys so long. It's no big deal. I'm trained. There was no danger. There was no contraindication, and I can always get a new one when the pain from that one goes away in a couple hours, right?" Kathleen was asking in staccato, pointing her right index finger, the one not hung up in the halo apparatus due to the multiple breaks. The back of her bed was inclined about thirty-five or forty degrees.

"And you are *not* supposed to have your bed tilted up or move your body around. We need to monitor your urine output. The catheter wasn't only a way to pee, you know. You claim you have all this training, but your head sure as *hell* ain't showing it. What am I supposed to do? I can't just write this all up as 'against medical advice'! How many of your over four hundred internal and external stitches will you rip out because you want to be a hardheaded dumbass tonight, huh?"

"Okay, okay. That's enough of doing things against orders and dumbass talk on both sides for one night!" I yelled above everybody else, which only brought on a cacophony of additional little whines and moans like kids on a playground.

"*Enough!*" I fairly screamed out.

Just then, Dr. Chen walked in for evening rounds.

"Maybe it's just a joke to you. You figure you have insurance to pay for most of it. All told, I spent almost twenty hours inside and outside you on your first day here at the hospital trying to get you back in one major piece. It would really piss me off if you undid any of my work," she yelled, punctuating each word by slapping the rail on the side of the bed with Kathleen's chart.

"Look, I know my rights..." began Kathleen, trailing off.

"Right now, you know exactly squat!" said Dr. Chen sharply.

"Kathleen, I know you're upset, but baby–" I began.

"Why don't you just shut up?" Kathleen shrilled at me.

My eyes got as big as saucers, and my jaw dropped open. I don't know whether I was more hurt or more amazed.

"Okay, I know that you're taking massive amounts of narcotics. And I know you're in a stressful situation right now. And I know there are two people dead that shouldn't be. But seriously, that is the most hateful, mean, terrible thing anybody has ever said to me in my life. When you can get word to me that you're sorry and you truly mean it, I'll be back but not one minute before. I love you more than there are stars in the summer sky, but I will not be subjected to this, and I will not put our unborn baby through the stress. Kathleen, before now, there was you and me. Now we have a baby. Everything we do, every way we act, we must do it for this baby. We've been planning for this, and now the time is here. The time is now! It pains me to say so, Kathleen, but you seriously need to get your shit in one bag and put it behind you while you have this contemplation, down time, or whatever you want to call it...time where you're off your feet. I'll do anything you need me to do. I'll be there every step of the way. But I will not have you acting ugly to me, or to anybody else for that matter."

I'd been there such short a time I'd not even put my purse down. I simply turned on my heel and walked out of the room in a daze. I wondered what had just happened. I know that Kathleen and I'd only been together for three years, but from the very start we had meshed like two jigsaw puzzle pieces. In the first week, we knew each other inside out. We finished each other's sentences. Heck, even when she tried to surprise me with my engagement ring I knew it was coming. Maybe everybody was right. Maybe this change in behavior was caused by the accident. What I did know was this: I wasn't going to live in this acrid atmosphere. I simply wasn't. Now, I...No! Now, *we* had a baby coming, and it was going to be raised in an atmosphere of joy and happiness.

※ ※ ※

Martha stood outside the ICU room for quite some time, drumming her fingers in the air as if on a desktop, stopping, then starting to gnaw on her index fingernail. She gathered her resolve and began to enter the room, then quickly stopped. She made several starts and stops, eventually heaving a large sigh, not knowing what to do.

"You know I can hear you out there, don't you, whoever you are?" said Kathleen.

Martha drew back the curtain and stepped into the room. She stood for a moment or two, wringing her hands, holding her keys, not knowing what to say, not knowing how to start, and not knowing how to open the ugly can of worms she had come to open.

"You know, you could sit down–" Kathleen started.

"Shut up! Kathleen, for once in your life I wish you would just shut up! When I signed on to the Pope family, I knew going in that I was on the second team, that I was a bench warmer. I knew that your mother was the saint, and I was a mere mortal. Occasionally, there were things left unsaid, and I shut my mouth. Occasionally, things were said that shouldn't have been, and I shut my mouth. I did it because I'm a team player. I know it's hard being a cop, so everything I can do to make it a little bit easier for Kevin, I'm willing to do that. And I know it's hard for you not having a mom…God knows I tried…and though you never really showed it, I hope I made a little bit of a difference. I hoped things had changed slightly in the past three years or so. They may or may not have, but I will tell you this: I consider Belladonna my own daughter as sure as if I'd given birth to her, so if you do anything else to hurt her, you'll find out just about how *fucking* far my fury can go! Get it?" she spat.

Kathleen sat motionless in her bed for multiple reasons, not the least of which was that this was the most emotion she had seen Martha display since she'd met her when she was barely older than fourteen. Hell and damn were the only words Martha used regularly, and Kathleen could only remember her saying shit a dozen times since she was fourteen.

"What the heck has gotten into you?" Kathleen sputtered, not able to move much in her bed, adequately argue, or yell back due to the maxillary mask in place over her broken facial bones.

"I'll tell you what's gotten into me, dammit! I've had to sit day after day, trying to find the words to get through to Bella and let her know there's nothing wrong with her. I want to let her know there's nothing wrong with her feeling the way she does because her wife is being a total and complete obfuscated bitch. You two had a way that you wanted your lives to be, and you were able to live that way. You two wanted to have a baby and presto! After very little trying, Bella gets pregnant. But now, life has thrown you a couple curveballs, which I might add is a lot fewer than most families get thrown, and you want to throw a hissy fit! And you want to take everything out on your wife. Well, I'm not going to have it! You can just pack that shit in, right here and right *fucking now*!"

Martha stood, feet shoulder width apart, hands on hips, one arm looped through her purse, and shirttail loose on one side from her gesticulating. A run through her hair with a brush would not have hurt at that moment.

"Martha!" laughed Kathleen.

"What?" screamed Martha.

"You said the 'F' word. I thought the only word you knew how to say was hell. Seriously, dammit and hell is all you ever said since I was little," Kathleen giggled.

"Well, keep it up and I might just say it some more!"

Kathleen started laughing, and the harder she laughed the funnier it got. That's kind of the standard thing when you're in a position where you hurt, and you can't laugh. Only in this case she was still taking narcotics for pain relief. The key to the game was to stay ahead of the pain and not get behind the guns. In laughing so hard, she allowed herself to get behind, and it got to be a struggle to catch up and maintain. Martha saw what was happening immediately and grabbed the nurse's call button from Kathleen, pressing it to call for help. Fortunately, there was a standing order for a relatively hardcore narcotic, and the wait time was very brief, but it would still be a while before Kathleen was able to overcome the pain.

"So, Martha, tell me, just so we're clear here. Were there a lot of those times…times where we said too much? Too little? Where *I* said too much or too little? Because for me, I mean, really, I guess it was more about being independent. I never had a mom growing up, so I've always been independent, and that's just what I knew. I don't know that I was willing to give up any of my independence."

"Honey, I wasn't asking you to give up any of your independence. And I wasn't asking you to let me be your mother. All I ever wanted was to just be Martha. And if you can accept that, then that is all I need; that was all I ever wanted. It just so happened that everything you needed help doing was boy stuff, and goodness knows I didn't really do any boy stuff. I only did woman and girl stuff because that's all I knew how to do."

Just then a nurse showed up carrying a large syringe and wearing an even larger smile.

"We had a pool going on when you'd want some more pain killers. You hadn't had any since last night at about eleven thirty. If ten o'clock had rolled around, we would have enforced the injection without asking," he said with a wide grin.

The nurse injected the contents of the syringe into the saline drip snaking into the back of Kathleen's hand. As was to be expected since Kathleen had really started hurting, relief was not going to be instantaneous.

"Just to let you know, your charts show that you might be getting some oral pain medications starting with meals, which means, you know what?" he said looking at them both expectantly, first one, then the other.

Martha and Kathleen looked at each other, not knowing what to say or think.

"Oh, come on, man! Think. That's a pretty good indication that they're going to start cleaning under the gauze and taking care of your face now. You're starting to heal. Before you know it, they'll give you a cane with wheels on it, so you can roll that halo around and cruise up and down the aisles. You'll be sweet trippin' up-and-down," he said, doing a little sashay of his own.

"Hey, Martha? Just for the sake of planning, whadd'ya say we neglect to mention our little tête-à-tête to Bella? Okay with you?"

Martha said nothing.

"And, Martha? One last thing. There's something I want to ask you…something I *need* to ask you. Those things that were said…Those things that weren't said…from me, I mean. Did I ever make you cry?" Kathleen asked in an almost tiny voice, so much unlike her usual self.

Again, Martha said nothing. For the longest time, Kathleen thought about how to reword the thought to readjust the question, but nothing came out of her mouth. After the nurse left and Martha had sat down in the chair, she quietly waited like any good mother would, watching over her child. Finally, at the end of the day, well after rush hour was over, which would make driving home easier, Martha once again got up and leaned over the bed to kiss Kathleen goodbye. Martha started to withdraw for the day but hesitated.

"To this day, I'm really not sure what anybody thinks of me, of my abilities, of how much I really love and care for this family, of the lengths that I would go to for anyone in this family…and I do mean anyone. It wasn't really given to me as a mission, as a message from me to you, but I'll tell you this: She loves you more than I love you or your father, and I could see that from the first day. She already loves that little baby as much as she loves you. It's part of you as far as she's concerned. Don't screw this up. If you're wondering why you haven't seen her in a day or so it's because she's not coming back...not until you've changed, not until you've sucked it up, and not until you want her back enough to tell her how sorry you are and really mean it. Now, maybe it's not my place to tell you that, but some things are a mother's job. As much as you may not like it sometimes, I still look at myself as your mother, no matter how poorly I fit your birth mother's shoes."

And with that, Martha bent down and kissed the back of Kathleen's good hand and left her room for the evening.

※ ※ ※

"Well, hello dear. Come on in. We certainly weren't expecting you tonight, not that you need an invitation or anything. You know, you're certainly welcome any time," Martha greeted Bella at her and Pops' front door, ushering her in warmly.

"I just happened to be driving by and thought I would bring a little show and tell."

After the big bear hug, Pops grabbed three mugs and put on a pot of coffee.

"Oh, Kevin. For the love of Pete! You, big lug! Babies don't drink coffee! What can I get you, dear? Maybe some orange juice or some weak green tea?" queried Martha.

"Oh, I forgot again," said Pops sheepishly.

"Oh, some orange juice would be just fine," I answered.

Since there was already some iced tea made up, Pops had that, and Martha had orange juice with me.

"So, what's this you brought by to show us? I just can't wait!" Martha cried out.

I reached into my purse and pulled out a bag of uncooked pinto beans. I pushed the package down flat with one bean all the way in the corner of the plastic package, then I grabbed it, pulling it through the edge of the plastic. I put that one bean in the middle of the table and pointed at it.

"Look at it!" I squealed, stamping my feet on the kitchen floor.

"Bells, sweetheart, it's a bean," Pops said rather dryly.

"Right now, that's how big your grandbaby is! Isn't it just the most exciting thing?" I exclaimed.

FURTHER INTO FIRE

"You know, nobody from my old neighborhood ever thought I'd have two daughters and grandkids to boot. Looks like I finally got bragging rights over this one," Martha said proudly.

"Look, Bella. I don't mean to pry..." Pops began.

"Anyway, that's all I have. I just thought it would be fun to show you that. Courtney's coming over tonight, so we can go over some stuff that has to be ready for a client meeting tomorrow. We just needed a little extra time to work on it. She's probably waiting on me now, so I better scoot. Love you both," I said, standing and grabbing my purse.

I had to keep going. I didn't want to turn around, and I didn't want them to see the tears threatening to stream down my cheeks. I knew in a matter of seconds they would be; nothing could stop them. Without really meaning to, I squealed the tires driving off. 'Well played, Bella. Well played,' I told myself in disgust.

❀ ❀ ❀

"Let's go get some dinner first. I'll drive," said Courtney.

"I can fix something here, if that's okay?" I replied.

"I want tacos, and that's the last of it. And I'm driving!"

"Yes, ma'am!"

We got in her car and drove through the drive-through, placing our order. But then, she took the wrong way out of the parking lot.

"Where are we going?" I asked.

"You'll see," she said, offering nothing else.

It began to dawn on me once she started driving to Minneapolis.

"Why are you driving over here?" I asked her pointedly.

"Because this is stupid. And it's going to stop right here and now. You love her, and she loves you, and it's plain stupid that the two of you aren't talking because of some stupid little thing."

"It's not little."

"In the big scheme of life, it's little. And for the sake of that creature in your belly, it's going to stop now!"

I let out the biggest of sighs, settled back in my seat, and grasped the bag of food tightly in my hands. I didn't see this meeting going well at all, regardless what outcome Courtney saw. Finally, we were in the parking garage at the hospital. We got out. I was carrying the food. At least we'd get to eat and pass some of the time not having to talk. We walked up the levels and down the hall to Kathleen's room. She was in her bed with the back tilted up in a semi-sitting position, which I'd not seen her in before, sleeping. Courtney and I both sat in chairs and quietly began eating our dinner.

"I'm an asshole," Kathleen quietly mumbled.
"What?" I asked.
"I'm an asshole," she repeated, somewhat louder.
"Why do you say that?"
"Because of the way I've been treating you. I'm sorry. You know that I love you more than life itself. I think the problem has been that life itself has been eluding me lately. I guess it's not my time to go after all. Do you forgive me?" she asked.

I started crying. This is the breakthrough I'd been hoping for, for weeks.

"Of course, I forgive you," I said, putting down my taco and approaching the bed on her good side, halfway straddling the bed and getting close to Kathleen.

"See? I told you so!" smarted off Courtney.
"How much can you see right now, Kathleen?" I asked.
"Some. Why?"

I dug down into my purse and got out the photos of the ultrasound. I held them up, so Kathleen could see them again.

"Our baby..." she said, as her eyes teared up, her left hand moving up, her fingers touching the pages.

"Are you happy?" I asked.
"Yes. Very."
"Then why are you crying?" I asked.
"I've been such a moron."
"That's in the past now, baby...in the past. Put it out of your head."
"How can you ever forgive me, Bella?"
"Forgive you? Because you're my wife, and I love you, and we're going to have a baby!"

I climbed up as far as I could on the bed and wrapped myself around Kathleen, feeling her body shake as she sobbed.

"Shhh, baby. It's all okay now. It'll all be all right!"

❦ ❦ ❦

"I told you it'd turn out okay, didn't I?" asked Courtney.
"You did at that."
"Now, how long do you think it's going to take you to remove that little smirk from your face?"
"What smirk?" I asked.
"The one you haven't been able to get off your cute little face since the hospital. You gonna wear it all day tomorrow at work? And don't

you think you owe it to Pops and Martha to tell them everything is okay?"

My head was so up in the clouds, I hadn't even noticed that she was driving to their house.

"You're devious," I said.

"And that's why I'm the very best administrative assistant you'll ever have!" she retorted.

Just then, we pulled into Pops' driveway and got out, rambling up to the porch. He must have heard the car because he met us at the open door.

"Everything good, girls? To what do I owe this wonderful visit?"

"Oh, Pops," I said as I wrapped him up in a giant hug.

"Whoa, must be something good."

"It is. Kathleen and I have made up. Everything is perfect. It was just…It was…Well, never mind. It's over now. Things are one hundred percent again. I showed her the photos of the ultrasound again, and she loves them!"

"That's wonderful! Come inside and have a cup of something with us!"

"Truly, we can't. We have work to do. I just wanted to stop and tell you, that's all."

"Well, come by any time. You know you girls are always welcome."

"I know, Pops. I love you. Tell Martha as well. Bye-bye."

And with that, we drove to my house to finally work on the next day's presentation. It was going to be a long night, but oh, so very worth it.

🌀 🌀 🌀

Lieutenant Reed was just walking into the room while I was sitting at Kathleen's bedside.

"Hi, Kathleen. Hi, Bella," he said in greeting.

We both echoed a hello.

"What brings you in, Reed?" asked Kathleen.

"Just a little news. The state police have finally got the insurance to replace the chopper. Heinelman's ribs and fingers have healed, and he has been cleared to fly again. One of the National Guard pilots has joined the team as his copilot, and they've hired him on as a temporary medic. They don't know how long they can hold your spot open. You're pretty banged up. Your long-term prognosis is hurry up and wait. You still have two weeks in your leg cast and about that much longer on your face piece. Your halo should come off in a month, maybe less. As far as your internal stuff…I have no idea."

"Look, Lieu. If you came to give me a pep talk, maybe you should go outside and work on it a while first, because you suck at it!" laughed Kathleen.

It was one of the few times I'd heard her laugh in weeks. It made my heart warm a little.

"You could always wait for a place on a Medic team, like you were before, especially if you can't pass a flight physical. I know it's not what you want, but I know you did love it. It's still all about saving people, right, Pope?"

"You're right, Reed. You're right. First, I have to make it out of this stupid bed. *And I want this stupid catheter out of me!*"

Just then a nurse entered carrying a walker.

"Well, this is your lucky day because that's what I'm here for. First, you're going to start using the walker to get yourself into the bathroom. I want you to use your left hand for power and your right hand with the halo *only* for balance. Do you hear me? Only for balance. I see you use it and its right back in bed with a bag and a tube. Still, if you have a problem and need help, don't hesitate to pull the help cord from the bathroom. If you have a problem near the bed, give the nurse call button a push. Now, if everybody will kindly shoo, we'll get you disconnected from this awful thing."

And with that Lt. Reed and I left the room to wander the hall for a moment. He was the nicest man, to be sure. He kept asking questions about Kathleen and Pops and Martha, all of whom he'd known for years.

"I have to tell you, Bella, I was surprised when Kathleen came and asked to take half a day off when you two went to the county offices to get your marriage license. I'd known she was gay forever, and everybody at the station knew about her tragedy with Melanie, but for you two to progress so fast was a miracle. And that it's lasted…Wow!" he said in awe.

"And guess what? I'm four months pregnant, too."

"Well, hot damn! That's good news! Is it for public consumption?" he asked.

"Yeah, I guess so."

"If you don't mind, I'd like to tell the guys down at the station."

"Sure, that'd be fine. It would be good news for a change. That, and let them know that Kathleen is genuinely doing better. In fact, tell them these exact words: 'As of today, Pope can take a shit on her own!' They'll get a kick out of that, I'm sure."

"I'm sure they will. Tell Kathleen bye for me. I have to get back to the station house," he said, giving me a great big hug and kiss on my cheek.

FURTHER INTO FIRE

❀ ❀ ❀

Martha and I came giggling into the hospital room about a quarter after six in the evening. Kathleen was sitting up in bed.

"Boy, have I got a surprise for you," I said.

"What's that," Kathleen replied.

"Let me take off this stupid goalie mask you wear, first," I said, unhooking the plastic straps, then removing the gauze over her lips and chin.

"What are you doing?" Kathleen asked, vehemently.

Martha handed over the jamocha milkshake she'd been hiding in her oversize purse, and I put the bendable straw in it that I'd brought from home.

"I thought you'd want a break from oatmeal and Jello. How's that hit the old spot, babe?"

Kathleen wasn't answering. She was sucking down on the straw for all she was worth. Finally, she stopped.

"Oh, my God! This is delicious! Why haven't you brought one sooner?"

"Because you were being a total bitch, and I don't reward bad behavior."

Kathleen's eyes started welling up and her body started shaking as she was silently crying.

"Oh, baby. I was just playing with you. Stop crying. Please. Baby, stop," I said as I dabbed at her eyes with a tissue.

She started sucking on her milkshake for a moment, then stopped again.

"It's true though. I have been. Completely."

I leaned into her, and as gently as possibly, I kissed her...for the longest time.

"Kathleen, being near death can do lots of strange things to people, and you coded multiple times. It totally tears through your emotions and turns them upside down. I get that. I do. So, let it go. I did the second you said that you were okay again. Gone in a second," I said to her, trying to convince her to let it go.

Kathleen's eyes continued to water, but she stopped shaking although she never stopped sucking on that delicious milkshake. In no time flat, she was sucking on air from the bottom of the cup. Just then, a nurse came into the room.

"Aha! Contraband!" she laughed.

I quickly threw the cup in the trash.

"Was it good, Kathleen?" she asked.

"It was flippin' marvelous after the crap they've been feeding me for the last few weeks," Kathleen said.

"Well, I won't tell if you won't," the nurse said.

The nurse proceeded to check all her vital signs, recording them in the chart.

"Are we ready to try and go to the bathroom again?"

"I guess so," Kathleen ventured.

The nurse placed her walker by the bed and let down the right side of the bed. Even though that was the side of Kathleen's broken leg, it was the side of her good arm for power. She managed to scoot off the bed, dangling her right leg, swinging her left foot around and putting that foot down, then putting her weight mostly on her left foot and some on her right. She used her right arm to push up on and her left arm just for balance, grabbing the walker. She made a lot of noise, grunting and groaning during the process. Finally, she was able to shuffle herself into the bathroom and sit down with her right leg out and her left leg bent in. It took her almost five minutes, but finally she was able to go. More grunts and groans followed as she was remounting the walker, getting back into the room, and finally got back into the bed. The look in her eyes was one of exhaustion.

Dr. Chen came into the room carrying a folder of x-rays.

"Hello, people. How is everybody?" she asked.

Everybody in turn said hello back to her.

"Let me show you what we've got. First, the left wrist...ready to come off in one week. Next, the right leg...ready to come off tomorrow afternoon. Ribs already healed. Face pretty much healed, but I still want to leave it in the plasti-mask for another month, just for protection; however, the gauze can come out. You can remove the mask to eat, but you must absolutely have it on for sleeping. And since you're up and going to the bathroom on your own, I'm going to recommend we get a home hospital bed and get you home healthcare. We need the bed here for patients, and I think you'll do a much better job, physically and emotionally, if you work from home. We'll have a nurse visit you every day, and starting next week, we'll have a physical therapist and occupational therapist start seeing you. What do you think about that?"

"Oh, baby, you'll be at home! I can see you all the time! And I can spoon feed you real food, not that shit they make you eat here!" I screamed.

"Actually, she will still be on a fairly restrictive diet," Dr. Chen said.

"We'll just see about that," I winked.

"Where will you put the bed?" asked Martha.

"I'll move the couch over against the windows and put it right downstairs. Probably wouldn't be very nice of me to make her walk upstairs yet, like she made me do when I was still crippled up."

"That was different," Kathleen croaked, half smiling.

"Was not!" I smiled back.

"Well, I'm glad to hear you are in such good spirits for a change," said Dr. Chen.

"I'd be in better spirits if I didn't have to go home to her," Kathleen said.

"Oh, now you're going to get it for real, baby. You are so going to get it," I grinned.

Kathleen was smiling more than I'd seen in a long time. Maybe, just maybe, we'd started turning the corner on this terrible thing.

❀ ❀ ❀

The next day, I called a home medical supply company and arranged for an immediate delivery. I ordered a bed, a table to roll over it, a free-standing and self-contained flush toilet, and a screen to hide it. They showed up promptly at ten thirty, and Ivan and Tinkerbelle showed interest in the new items at exactly ten thirty-one. You know what they say about curiosity and cats? That certainly describes both of our cats. Neither of them ever tried to go outside, so the open door wasn't a problem, but getting underfoot a bit was. I was just going to shut them in the bedroom upstairs when the medical company guys got the bed situated in place downstairs, so I didn't have to. They placed the stand-alone flush toilet near the bed and placed a folding three-panel screen around it. They also set a folding walker at the end of the bed within easy reach. As I signed the paperwork and the two men left, both Ivan and Tinkerbelle jumped up on the bed and rolled around, purring their little hearts out.

I know the bathroom area was sort of open, but it would allow Kathleen to come home; she'd be out of the hospital. Even with dietary restrictions, I could start her on 'normal' food and help her eat at night. The nurse would be with her during the day, and I would be home with her every single night. It had been a long two months. I had gone from being oh so afraid she was going to die, to a period where I think she didn't want to live, to having her back with me. My baby was nearly by my side again. And today after her cast was removed, she'd be brought home by ambulance. She would be accompanied by a nurse for the first afternoon and evening, and thereafter only during the days.

It was nearly lunch time, and I went into the kitchen to make our favorite: a cotto salami on wheat bread sandwich with green goddess dressing and sliced tomatoes. I ate half with some cheese curls and drank a soda. I set the plate down on the coffee table alongside the couch and lay down. As I did, my eyes slowly drifted shut. The last thing I remember was watching the cats curled up and sleeping on the hospital bed.

Suddenly, there was a pounding on the door. I jumped up with a start, running for the door. It was one of the ambulance attendants.

"We're here with Kathleen Pope?"

"Oh, sorry," I said, rattled from having been startled out of my sleep.

I stepped back and opened the door wide, while the attendant blocked open the storm door. He walked back to the ambulance, and the two men pulled the gurney out of the back, lowering the wheels. They pulled Kathleen gently out of the back of the ambulance and brought her to the steps of the house. Partially collapsing the wheels, they brought her up onto the porch, then extended them once again. They maneuvered her through the door and alongside the hospital bed. They then grabbed the sheet on the gurney and lifted her over onto the bed.

"Well, look at you! No more cast," I exclaimed.

"Yeah, finally. It feels good to get it off. My muscles suck, and I can't put any weight on it, but it'll get there eventually. I'll build it up going to the bathroom. What's behind the screen?"

"Your bathroom," I replied.

"Oh, no, no, no! That's not happening."

"It's just for now. And it flushes like an RV toilet, so it's just fine. You'll do what you have to do. Don't make me kick you in the head. And besides, you had community toilets in the army. Remember?"

"I was never in the army. What are you talking about?"

"Joking, baby. Joking."

"Any other good news you have for me?"

"Want half a cotto salami sandwich before the nurse gets here?"

"Have I told you how much I love you?"

"I thought that might change your mind. Let me get your mask off," I said as I hurriedly started undoing her elastic.

"Ma'am, if I could just get you to sign here, we'll be out of your hair," said the paramedic.

"Oh, sure. There you go."

"You two ladies have a wonderful afternoon."

"Thank you, gentlemen for bringing my wife home to me," I said, garnering a look from the two men as they took their gurney back to the ambulance and drove away.

FURTHER INTO FIRE

I pulled off bite-sized pieces of the sandwich for Kathleen, who was ravenous, and we finished just as the nurse showed up at the door and pushed the bell.

"Hi. I'm Bella Pope. And this is Kathleen."

"Hi there. My name is Minnie Logan. I guess I'll be with you for the next few weeks. Now then, I've already been told you're a bit of an ornery one. Well, I'm not going to have any of that. What I say goes. I'm the boss while I'm here. Don't mean I'm a tyrant, just means I'm in charge! And I'm going to take special good care of you. You'll see that. Now, first things first. Here in my bag I've got a banana, a peach, a pear, and an apple. Which one do you want me to go cut up for you? Not going to be any junk food here. Fruit is what's good for you. Tomorrow, I better see a big old basket of it on the counter!" she said as she took off her sweater and set her things down, walking toward Kathleen as she spoke.

"I'm really not that hungry right now, to tell you the truth," spoke Kathleen.

"Girl, what did I just tell you? I'm the one in charge. You need a snack to keep your energy up and get all better. Now, either you choose, or I'll just go cut one up and come back and feed you."

I couldn't help but laugh out loud, which irritated Kathleen. I think she'd finally met her match. I'm sure this elderly woman had a heart of gold, but she had a fist of iron. No room for slackers at all. Minnie took off the mask for the second time when she returned from the kitchen with the apple cut up into small bites. She set the plate on Kathleen's right side, so she could reach it.

"Lordy, child, for somebody who wasn't particularly hungry, you sure cleaned that plate like a vacuum cleaner on high speed!" Minnie laughed.

I couldn't help it. I joined in. Kathleen even gave a small grin at that one. For as mean and blustery as she blew in the door, Minnie did indeed possess the most charming personality. She was old school, and like a teacher on the first day of school, she demanded respect, and she marked her spot like an alpha dog. She was a sweetie deep down. I gave her a key to our house, so she could let herself in every day and told her I'd have lunch made from the previous night's dinner and save it in the refrigerator for both her and Kathleen. She objected, but I insisted. She objected again, but I told her that I already heard about her being ornery, and I was in charge. She laughed. I asked her if there were any dietary restrictions. She said nothing too spicy and everything had to be healthy food for Kathleen.

After Miss Minnie was gone, I told Kathleen I had a couple of surprises for her. She asked what, but I just went upstairs and came down with a few things and set them down. I went in the kitchen and filled up a small dish tub with warm water and body wash. I went back to Kathleen's bed and took off her mask for the third time since she was home, placing it on the shelf.

"What are you doing?"

"Roll over on your left side."

She did the best she could and reached behind her and untied the hospital gown she was still wearing. I rolled her back over and took it off her, then began to gently clean her face with the sponge I had brought with me. When I was done I had her first roll left, cleaning her back, her bottom, her legs, and her feet. Then I had her roll right and repeated the task. When I had finished that, I began to slowly work my way down from her chest, taking a little more time than I should on her breasts.

"You know, we've been together for three and a half years now, and I still get excited every time I see your boobs. Do you know that?"

"Stop. Don't make me laugh."

"What? It's true, baby," I said, lightheartedly.

I kept working my way down her body, all the way to her feet, then leaned over her and took her right nipple into my mouth, biting it playfully, flicking my tongue over the tip of it.

"Quit that!"

"Quit what? This?" I asked as I put the sponge down and moved my right hand over the thickly-populated hair at the juncture of her legs and ran my fingers through it, not letting up on her nipple.

"Damn it, Bella. Stop that!"

"You mean stop this?" I asked as I moved my index finger lower, parting her, beginning to rub her in a gentle, circular motion, applying just enough pressure.

"No," were her words, but her right hand grabbed a handful of my hair and pulled my head tightly to her breast, holding on for dear life. It didn't take more than about fifteen minutes of me stimulating her, suckling her, and her grabbing my hair, pulling on me while at the same time forcing my head down tightly, for her hips to buck off the bed. She went stiff as a board, occasionally slamming back down on the bed, then immediately coming up in the air again for an extended period. After seven or eight minutes, she managed to gasp out one word....

"Stoooop."

I stopped all motion. I didn't move my hand from her, but I did lift my head and lay it down on her chest, listening to her heart race a hundred miles an hour. We lay like that for nearly half an hour while she dozed off. Finally, her eyes fluttered open.

"Baby, are you all right? Did I make you hurt anywhere?"

"Not too much. Why did you insist on doing that?"

"Why can't I make love to my beautiful wife? It's called being in love."

"I'm not beautiful."

"You *are* beautiful; you just look awful."

"And what do you mean by that?"

"You haven't had any regular food for almost three months now. You haven't been to the gym. You've lost over twenty-five pounds. You're still you, but you're not in fighting shape. You'll get back. It'll just take time. I'll say this, though, you've still got the sexiest legs this side of the Mississippi river! They're responsible for us being together now. At least, they sped up the process. I can still remember the first time we made love in my old apartment. In the hospital, you stole my breath away. In my bed, you stole my heart away that first day."

Looking down at herself, still lying naked in the bed, Kathleen started frowning.

"I've never thought I was beautiful. I mean, I was okay with how I looked, but now I'm scarred from head to toe. I feel like it makes me ugly somehow."

"Remember the day we were up in the Iron Range? We saw twenty oak trees lined up in a row. All of them were nearly identical to each other, but on one somebody had carved a heart out of the bark and put the inscription 'GH +TR 4VR.' That could be considered an imperfection by some, but it's what made *that* tree the special one because it was different. No other tree in the world is like that one. Do you understand how I feel about you? Baby? Those scars are your merit badges. They stand for how you lived through something that killed two other people. For God's sake, a piece of the helicopter sliced through your stomach and only your physical conditioning kept you from dying. Do you hear what I'm saying to you? Do you?"

"I guess...."

"You guess?" I said, raising an eyebrow and getting right in her face, leaning in for a long, lingering kiss.

It was our first since the accident, our first true, lasting, lovers' kiss. I moved the tub and sponge to the kitchen, came back, and sat on the side of the bed.

"And now, my next surprise. Lift up your feet."

Puzzled, she did as she was told. I picked up a pair of shorts from the floor where I had dropped them and slipped them over her feet. As I began to move them up over her, she kept raising up parts of her body until they were fully up around her waist, and she was smiling like the Cheshire cat.

"Real clothes. I like this surprise."

"And you didn't like the last one?"

"Answer me this: Did you plan on making love to me, or did that just happen?"

"I've been planning it for three days," I said, grinning at her.

"I wish I could return the favor…" she said with a bit of a sad look on her face.

"Baby, we've got the rest of our lives. You worry too much."

I picked up a St. Paul Fire Department tee shirt and a pair of scissors.

"What in the hell are you doing?" Kathleen said with a bit of terror in both her voice and her eyes.

"I'm going to cut the bottom of the sleeve, so it will go over your halo."

"Try it before you cut my good tee shirt!"

"Kathleen, I got out the oldest, rattiest one I could find. You must have thirty of them! Now, stop!" I said as I cut the sleeve.

She lay there with her mouth agape as if I'd kicked her dog, but I held out my arm and told her to pull up on it, so she could sit up. She had trouble getting up, but she'd have to get used to it. I slipped the cut arm over her halo first, then guided her head through and finally, threaded her right arm through.

"No offense, but I think real clothes is better than the sex," she said, cackling and rubbing her chest, feeling the smooth cotton shirt and smiling broadly.

"Fine, I'll remember that tomorrow night when I–," I started.

"I take it back! I take it back!" she screamed, reaching for me as I stood up from the bed.

"Think you might want to take another little nap while I go fix dinner?"

"Would you bring me my music player?"

"Okay. Back in just a few."

I picked up the scissors and took them upstairs with me, putting them away while I got her player. Just out of curiosity, I turned it on. It was dead. Of course, it hadn't been charged in months. I picked up mine instead and took that one to her.

"This one is yours. Where's mine?"

"On the charger, that's where yours is. She's dead."

"Oh. Yeah. I guess."

I leaned over her and kissed her forehead and began to walk away, but she grabbed me by the bottom of my blouse and spun me around. Even out of shape, this woman was tremendously powerful.

"I'm afraid that won't do it," she explained.

I smiled as I turned back to her and again leaned over her and kissed her deeply and passionately, like a lover.

"Your music is crap," Kathleen complained.

"How can that be? It's ninety-eight percent the same as yours."

"Well, the other two percent is crap."

I giggled to myself as I went into the kitchen to cook our dinner and tomorrow's lunch for her and Miss Minnie. I made dry rub barbequed boneless skinless chicken breasts and fresh green beans.

"Hey, Kathleen, just for tomorrow, you're going to have the same thing for lunch, but this weekend I'll cook several things, so you'll have a choice, okay? The same way you did for me when we first met and you were taking care of me. Baby?" I hollered from the kitchen.

She didn't answer, so I poked my head around the corner. Her ear buds were in, her head was bobbing, and her foot was bouncing to the music. This woman could bring a smile to my face in so many ways. I walked back into the kitchen and did what I would do more and more the coming months, I patted my stomach where I was beginning to really show. I never had a six-pack like Kathleen, but I do, er, that is I did have a flat stomach. I was really beginning to show.

Before long, dinner was ready. I cut it up in small bites, so Kathleen could eat it on her own. I knew she would want to, being the independent cuss that she is. I brought our plates into the living room with a glass of tea for both of us, and I sat down in the chair by the bed. She was still rocking to the tunes.

"Love muffin," I said softly, but got no reaction.

I could hear the music blaring even with the earbuds in her ears. I tugged them loose.

"Are you trying to make yourself deaf?" I yelled.

"What?" she yelled back.

We both broke into an uncontrollable laughing fit. It's amazing how much better Kathleen had become in just the past three or four days and coming home had just intensified that. And, truth be told, the sex didn't hurt. I set her plate on the bed and handed her a fork, and then put a hand towel on her chest to catch any falling food since it was a long way between the plate and her mouth.

"So, do you want to get into a fight tonight?" I asked.

"Why do you ask that?"

"So we can have some really good make-up sex," I said with a grin.

"Oh, you're a funny girl. A regular Bob Hope," she said, taking a bite.

"I'm just saying," I said, taking a bite myself.

"Truthfully? After laying in that bed for months, even though I was only conscious for part of the time, I *really* needed that!"

"I thought you might. Anyway, I thought it couldn't hurt. And I was prepared to stop if you truly weren't receptive. But when you jerked my hair out by the roots, I figured it was a lock."

"Don't be crass," she said, stuffing more food in her mouth.

I'd hate to get between her fork and her face. I'd get stabbed for sure! After dinner, I loaded the dishwasher and then went upstairs to change into my jammies. After I brushed my teeth and took off my makeup, I went back downstairs to Kathleen and told her to scoot over in her bed. It didn't have the most room in the world, but I wanted to get next to her for just a little bit before an early bedtime.

"I have to be in earlier than normal in the morning for a staff meeting. I'm going to catch up on a couple of things and work a little late since you'll have your babysitter here tomorrow."

"I'll be sure and tell Miss Minnie you think of her as a babysitter."

"You'll do no such thing!" I sternly told Kathleen.

"Do you know how good this feels, to be home and with you here, right now? And to have you sleeping just upstairs?"

"Kathleen? I'm going to say something, and I'm going to say it just once. I want you to listen good."

"What, honey?"

"Don't ever, ever, ever shut me out again."

"Look–"

"You nearly broke my heart those three weeks. It was like you reached into my chest with your hand and ripped it right out. I would never be able to take that again."

Even though her right arm was sort of trapped, she brought it up and started caressing me with her hand.

"I promise you, as God is my witness, I will never do it again. I swear it."

"Okay. Let's never speak of it again then. Since tomorrow is Friday, I'm going to stop and get some walleye and home fries on the way home. How about that?"

"Sounds good to me."

"Okay, time for your mask to go back on. For goodness sake, don't let Miss Minnie know it was off almost all night. She might have a conniption fit. And if she makes you wear it except for lunch, don't give her any shit about it. Okay?"

"Yes, Mom."

I slapped her leg for that comment. Her beautiful, sexy leg. Just as I was getting up to go upstairs it sounded like a herd of buffalo were running past. It was Tinkerbelle and Ivan running down the staircase. They ran to the bottom and immediately jumped into the bed with Kathleen, who was so happy to see them both. They purred for her and were walking around on her, and she reached out as far as she could and scratched them both, making them purr even louder.

"Good night, lover. I'll see you in the morning," I said, giving her one last kiss before heading up to bed.

I couldn't help but think that this was one step closer to having Kathleen in bed with me every night, and that certainly brought a smile to my face. Looking at my nightstand, I saw I had forgotten one thing. I picked it up and walked back downstairs.

"Couldn't stay away from me, could you?" Kathleen laughed.

"Not exactly. One last present," I said, extending my hand to her, palm up, holding the object.

"What's this? Oh, a bell. Perfect. I hadn't even thought about that. Now, I won't have to shout through the house."

"But I know you. You're so damned independent, you won't use it unless you absolutely have to. I want you to promise me that you'll use it if you need anything at all."

"I will."

"Kathleen!"

"Okay, I promise."

"Goodnight, baby. I love you. I'm so glad you're home."

"I love you too. And I'm glad to be here."

※ ※ ※

I was startled awake by a noise downstairs. I couldn't figure out what it was at first. I threw back the covers and sprinted downstairs, flipping on lights as I went. I found Kathleen standing alongside her bed, grunting.

"What is it? What's the matter?" I asked, frantically.

"Leg cramps."

I started laughing at her. I just couldn't help it. I was so worried and here she was, almost comical.

"It's not funny!"

"No, baby, it's not. I was panicked that something was really wrong. I'm just relieved. Here, let me help you. Which leg?"

"My right one."

The one that had been broken. I knelt at her feet and began to deep massage her calf with both of my hands. I could feel the severe knots. After about two minutes, they magically let go. I kept it up for several more minutes though. Finally, I asked Kathleen if she didn't want to slip back in bed.

"Jesus...Christ...That was painful," she replied as she sat down on the side of the bed.

I finally convinced her to lie down. When she did, she scooted all the way to the right side of the bed and laid her arm across her pillow.

"Lay down with me, please," she pleaded.

"Of course. Why wouldn't I?" I offered in return.

I got in bed with her, laying my head on her arm with the halo, spooning up against her. As soon as I did, her right arm reached over and started rubbing my stomach.

"Are you saying I'm starting to get fat?" I laughed.

"I noticed this afternoon, you're really beginning to show."

"I should be. I'm over four months along now. I'm surprised I don't show a little more."

"I want something," she asked with a hesitancy in her voice.

"What's that, baby?" I asked.

"Not now, but maybe in about two or three years."

"What would you want in about two or three years?" I asked quizzically.

"A baby. I want to have a baby. I know it may not be possible because of the crash, but I want to try."

"Kathleen Pope! I thought you never wanted to have children of your own and that was my duty!"

"I've changed my mind."

"You know what? Underneath your gruff exterior and all those muscles, you're just a little girl after all. Ha ha."

She hugged me tightly to her and continued to rub my stomach until we were both asleep. I had forgotten that I didn't have my alarm clock with me. It just never occurred to me when I got in bed with Kathleen, but about ten minutes before it would have gone off, Kathleen shook me and told me I probably needed to get up. I looked at my watch, and sure enough, it was. I guess after so many years of being a firefighter she had a built-in time clock or something. I turned over and kissed her hungrily, wishing I could stay right there with her and spend the day, but I had obligations I couldn't duck this particular Friday.

As I dashed out the door, I reminded Kathleen that lunch was in the refrigerator and admonished her to follow Miss Minnie's orders. She promised me she would, and I was off for a hectic day at the office. I leaned in for one last lurid, slow kiss, then it hit me that I hadn't gotten Kathleen her breakfast. Shit. I dropped my purse and briefcase, went into the kitchen, and quickly cooked some eggs and toast then poured some juice. I fed Kathleen, trying not to hurry her, but she understood the rush and pretty much wolfed down her breakfast in response, for which I was appreciative. Finally, I jumped in my SUV and drove off to the office.

The key turned in the lock at about nine o'clock. Miss Minnie's head peered around the door.

"Good morning, Kathleen. How are you on this wonderful Friday morning?" she asked gleefully.

"I'm doing pretty well. How are you?"

"Oh, just wonderful. Give me about another hour for my joints to start working and I'll be doing okay. At my age, not everything works like it used to," she said with a big throaty laugh.

That made Kathleen laugh as well. She could tell that she and Minnie would get along well.

Kathleen had kicked her sheet off for comfort and was laying there in her shorts and tee shirt. Minnie picked up on that right away.

"Look at you, all dressed up to go to a party! Don't you hate those awful hospital clothes? They leave your backside just hanging in the breeze for everybody and their dog to see!"

Again, Kathleen laughed. It was something she would do a lot with Minnie by her side over the next weeks. As they were eating lunch, Minnie feeding Kathleen even though it was the same meal she had fed herself the night before, Minnie had gotten a gleam in her eye and said nothing for several minutes.

"What? You act like you want to say something," Kathleen prompted her.

"Oh, it's nothing much. I was just remembering. You triggered something that I hadn't thought about in many, many years."

"Tell me. I want to know," Kathleen said wantonly.

"Well, okay, but it's just between you and me, child. Right?"

"Right. Got it."

"I was married to my Wilfred for forty-two years before I lost him, God rest his soul. But before that, while I was in nursing school...one of my classmates...her name was Lucinda. We got along famously. Now, keep in mind, this was a long time ago. Not like it is today. More scandalous, don't you know. And I'm black and she was white, which was unheard of..." she began.

"You and Lucinda?" Kathleen asked, incredulously.

"Oh, we were so in love. It lasted the entire time we were in nursing school. I believe the current term is 'gay until you graduate'? I thought we would last forever. We were in Chicago. I got a job locally, but Lucinda had always wanted to go to New York, so she took a vacation there before she looked for a job. I got a letter a month later that said she'd gotten a job in New York, met a doctor, and they'd fallen in love. It broke my heart. But then, I met Wilfred, and he fixed it. I don't think I was gay. I think I just saw the person and that's what I was in love with. Wilfred knew about Lucinda and told me that he was just the medicine to get me over her," she said with a laugh.

"I'm glad you told me that. That's a special story."

"I can tell you have a special one in Bella by the way she looks at you constantly. You couldn't have chosen better."

"I have to tell you, while I was in the hospital we didn't even see each other for three weeks. I froze her out. I don't even know why. I sort of went crazy in the head. I don't know what came over me. But apparently, she's forgiven me. We don't talk about it, but she told me that if I ever did it again I'm out on my ass. Plain and simple."

"Then I suggest, young lady, you never do it again," she said with a big, toothy grin.

"You're telling me!"

"Now stop all this talking and finish your lunch. It's getting cold, and besides, I want to go get my lunch. I'm an old lady, and I need my energy," she laughed.

Miss Minnie did that a lot. She laughed from the minute she stepped in the door until the minute she left. On her way out the door, she tickled Kathleen under the chin.

"God bless you, child. I'll see you on Monday. The bad news is you've got a couple of visitors starting on Monday—physical and occupational therapy. Physical in the morning, and occupational is going to make you start eating on your own and helping you with going to the bathroom, even though you're already doing that. They want to make sure you're using your body correctly. Embarrassing, but necessary. You have a great weekend, darling. Okay?"

"Okay, you too. Be safe."

"I'll say a prayer for you both in church on Sunday. Bye-bye."

And with that the key turned in the lock once again, and she was gone for the weekend.

It was almost seven o'clock when Kathleen heard the key in the door again. She was beginning to get hungry and wondering when I was going to get home. I walked in, dropped my purse, briefcase, and sack of food, and then kicked my shoes off by the door. I then started unbuttoning my blouse seductively and dropped it at the foot of the bed. I unbuttoned my pants and slid them down my legs, letting them pool at my feet. I slipped my socks off and flung them across the living room. Kathleen just watched, saying nothing, her eyes getting bigger by the moment. I unhooked my bra but held it in place with my arms, leaned forward, then moved my arms, letting it fall. Finally, I hooked my fingers into my panties, slid them down to my ankles, and kicked them loose.

"Ooo-kay. I'm impressed. And this is for?" Kathleen stuttered.

I moved up over the foot of the bed and grabbed Kathleen's shorts and pulled them down and off. I leaned forward and began playing with her with my tongue and fingers until she was rising off the bed and moaning. I kept this up for over three quarters of an hour until she had achieved ecstasy not only once but three times. Then I crawled up next to her and shoved her to the right-hand side of the bed, so I could spoon with her again. I took her right hand and placed it between my legs. She took the cue, and soon, I was pleased as well. As we lay there basking in the afterglow, it was Kathleen who was first to speak.

"Not that I'm complaining, mind you, but what brought all that on?"

"I've been horny since I woke with you this morning. I'm surprised the people in the conference room this morning couldn't smell me. My, God! What you do to me, Kathleen!"

"Mike told me about this with his wife. The entire time she was pregnant she fucked him like a rabbit. Is this what I have to look forward to?"

"I don't know. Maybe. Would that be so bad?"

"Just so long as you don't cut me off when the baby is born."

"I wish you could come with me on Tuesday for the second ultrasound. Martha's been great though. I just wish you two had bonded years ago. It almost seems like wasted time."

"I know. It was just timing though. And I've got to tell you, like I said before, it was like she was just trying too hard. She changed when you came along. I swear she did. Way for the better."

"Erm...If you'll take your fingers out of me now, I'll warm up the walleye and fries. I'm sure it's cold by now," I laughed.

Kathleen withdrew her fingers and put them in her mouth as I watched with my peripheral vision. It made me want to make love to her all over again, but I had to get up and deliver us some sustenance. Damn! I hated being responsible sometimes.

※ ※ ※

The physical therapist was working with strap-on weights and having Kathleen do leg lifts both front and back while holding four-pound weights in her hands. She was even using her hand with the halo, lifting in different directions. She kept telling the physical therapist that the weights were so light that she wasn't getting any resistance at all. She was used to hundred-pound weights. The physical therapist told Kathleen it wasn't about how much weight at this point, it was about starting over. This was really beginning to annoy Kathleen and was eating at her patience. She decided she was going to have me bring her weights to play with in the evening and then, I would take them into the office where they wouldn't be seen when she was done.

All in all, though, she had to admit that she really hurt by the end of the hour-long workout. The last thing the therapist did was to rub massage oil thoroughly into her legs from top to bottom and her arms from her biceps to her forearms. That alone was worth the price of admission. It made her feel wonderful. Maybe the girl knew her stuff after all.

If she thought she was annoyed with the physical therapist, it was nothing compared to her feelings for the occupational therapist. She thought the woman was going to drive her nuts with her condescension. Kathleen wasn't mentally deficient, she was a convalescent. When the woman wanted to have her cut up her own food, she flat out told her that the halo held her wrist in place, immobilized, keeping her from moving her hand.

"You do understand the purpose of a halo, don't you?" Kathleen asked sharply.

"Oh, I guess I didn't realize. I thought it just supported your wrist. I didn't think. My apologies," she mumbled weakly.

'I guess somebody makes up the bottom quarter of their class, and in this case it's you!' Kathleen thought to herself.

She showed the woman she could eat. The woman also started talking about her dressing herself. Kathleen just sighed. She used her good hand to snake that arm out of her tee shirt. Then she used it to pull her head out, although struggling with it a bit. Then she pulled out her left arm. When she was done, she managed to get her shirt right-side-out and reversed the process. She wished she had on a bra at that moment, but figured what the hell, she was going to have to do it. When it came to her shorts, she merely swung her feet off the bed, slid her shorts down with her right hand, pulled them back up, and got back in bed.

"Satisfied?"

"I know some of what I'm having you do may seem childish, but it all has a purpose. I wish you wouldn't be cross with me. I'm on your side,

I really am. I'm here to make sure you have all the life skills needed as you recover to be fully self-sufficient, dear."

'Dear? Ugh. God give me the strength,' thought Kathleen.

The last thing she had to do was use the toilet. She had anticipated this and had already decided she would just stay clothed and 'simulate' the process. The only hitch was, she really had to pee. She grabbed the walker, went around the screen, pulled down her shorts, and sat down. The woman was still watching her, however.

"Would you mind stepping to the other side of the screen now? I think I have it from here," Kathleen said rather huffily.

"Oh, of course," she said, stepping back.

Kathleen still felt like she was on display. She couldn't help but think about Miss Minnie sitting happily on the couch all morning, reading her magazines and her bible, humming to herself. She wouldn't mind if Minnie had stood there at all. She really liked Minnie and had only known her since last Thursday. How strange to develop an attraction in such a short time. It gave her an idea.

After everybody had gone for the day, she picked up her phone and called me.

"Hey, sweetie."

"Hey, baby. How are you doing? How was therapy?"

"Sore. Very sore. Lying around for three months has made me soft. I'm used to hours a week at the gym or downstairs."

"I know you are, but you'll get back there. Just give it time. Social call, or do you need something?"

"I need something. I need you to stop on the way home and get a music player. Nothing with a huge capacity," she said.

"Okay. I can do that. I won't be too late tonight."

"Are you going to rape me again tonight?" she asked.

"No, I don't think so. I think I'm all right today," I laughed heartedly out loud.

"Damn. I was hoping."

"I didn't say I wouldn't make love to you," I whispered through the phone just as Courtney walked past.

"I heard that, you nasty thing. I may try that myself tonight."

"Hey. Eavesdropping is a federal crime!" I laughed at her.

"But it's so fun!" she laughed back.

"What was that?" asked Kathleen.

"I just got busted by Courtney."

"Well, we're married. It's allowed."

"Yes, we are. We're married. Imagine, it's been three glorious years, and we're still on our honeymoon."

"All because a stupid Texas girl didn't know how to walk on the ice," mused Kathleen.

"I'm so glad I didn't. So glad. Have I told you lately how sexy your legs are? I want you back in the gym to get them back in full form. You have the sexiest legs on the planet."

"Oh, puh-leaze!"

"I have to run. I'll see you tonight. I won't forget to stop off for you either. Love you."

"I love you too, Bella."

After dinner, Kathleen started loading music up on the player.

"You never told me what that's for. Yours is working, it just needed to be charged," I said.

"This is for Miss Minnie. I'm downloading gospel music for her, so she can listen to it while she's here and reading her magazines and her bible. I thought it would be nice."

"That's so sweet. You know, I've always thought you had a heart of gold."

※ ※ ※

I was still home in the morning when Minnie came, since I was going for my ultrasound. Kathleen had her put the earbuds in and queued up Mahalia Jackson. Minnie fairly crooned as Kathleen hoped she would.

"I'll teach you how to use it if you don't already know," Kathleen said.

"My grandson and my daughter live with me. He has two of these things. I always thought they were silly, but it was because of the so-called music he listens to. This is delightful."

"I got it for you. I want you to have it. I thought you could listen to it when you read your bible or your magazines. I've already loaded it up with a ton of gospel music. And of course, we can pick out other music during the day while you're here, if you want to."

"Lord, I don't know what to say...You did this for me? I feel blessed. I truly do," she said as she leaned over the bed and gave Kathleen a big hug.

"Well, girls, I hate to run, but I have an appointment with the photographer," I laughed.

"You gonna get your portrait done?" asked Miss Minnie.

"No, my second ultrasound is today," I responded, full of joy and smiling broadly.

"Well, have fun," said Minnie.

"See you later, sweetie," said Kathleen, holding her arms open for me.

I leaned down and gave her a deep kiss and left to go pick up Martha.

At the clinic, they got me on the table, pulled my pants down a ways, pulled my shirt way up, and squirted the ultrasound goop all over my belly. I was growing fast. It seemed like I'd grown just in the last week. I wasn't imagining it, I'd actually grown; they'd measured me with a tape before putting me down on the table. Martha was all enthusiastic. As the technician started, she was looking for the overall image of the baby before taking all the measurements.

"Sorry, still not in any position to tell the sex."

"That's okay. I don't mind either way," I said happily.

But as she was taking measurements, suddenly, the baby flipped over, and *it* came into view.

"Well, I take that back, Mrs. Pope. It's a boy!"

Martha squeezed my hand.

"Kevin Steven Pope," I exclaimed.

She squeezed it several more times.

"He'll appreciate that…they both will. You know that."

"I hope so."

After we left the clinic, we stopped back at our house first since it was fairly close.

I walked over to the bed and took out the photos. I showed her three of them first, then showed her the one showing the sex last.

"A boy! Pops will jump up in the air! I mean, he would have liked either one, but he doesn't know we're naming him Kevin," Kathleen said as she teared up.

"How about we get them over here tonight and tell him. Martha promised not to rat us out."

"That sounds great."

I showed them to Minnie as well, who thought he was precious. I took the photo that she'd managed to quickly capture while the tiny penis was showing, wrote his name on the top in a black marker, then scanned it in. I immediately sent it via email to Mama, Daddy, Bryce, and Nancy. I picked up my phone.

"Courtney Braun. May I help you?"

"It's a boy!"

"Wonderful!"

"Now, get back to work. I have to go."

"Okay. Thanks for calling," she laughed into the phone.

"Are you going to be here tomorrow afternoon?" Minnie asked me.

"I hadn't planned on it. Why?"

"They're going to pick up Kathleen in a mobility bus and take her to the hospital. They called about a half hour ago. They changed the schedule. They're going to take off her halo tomorrow at two fifteen. They'll pick her up at one o'clock. You can ride the bus with her if you want. They'll bring a wheelchair for her."

"Hey, Kathleen. You want to see something totally bizarre?" I asked her.

"What?"

I turned sideways to her and lifted my blouse up, not pushing my stomach out intentionally.

"Holy shit! It hasn't even been a week! Look at you!"

"I know. Is that weird or what? I had started to worry because I wasn't showing that much. Can you believe it? I feel like I sat down to Thanksgiving and ate half a turkey!"

I picked up my phone again.

"Could I please speak to Lieutenant Pope? It's his daughter-in-law, Bella. Yes, I'll hold."

"Hi, Bells. What's going on?"

"Bring Martha over to our place tonight after dinner for some coffee and donuts. You aren't busy, are you?"

"No, nothing planned. We'll be there about seven or seven thirty, okay?"

"Okay, Pops. See you then."

Then my phone rang.

"Kevin Steven Pope?"

"Hi, Daddy. What do you think? You don't like the name?"

"I love the name…even if I don't get top billing," he laughed at me with a huge laugh.

"I thought you might. I love you, Daddy," I said with affection.

"I love you too, Doodles. I love you too. I have to run. Talk to you soon."

When I got to work that afternoon, people were congratulating me. Up until that point, I'd not mentioned to anybody that I was pregnant. Courtney and her big mouth! She'd sent emails to the entire company! Her desk is just outside my office.

"You, bitch, are in big time trouble. I may have you sacked."

"You wouldn't dare. You love me."

"Yes, I love you, but for that little stunt I would have a bullet put through the back of my brother's head!"

She laughed the whole afternoon intermittently. We talked here and there over the phone about business matters, but finally she came into my office and plopped down with a shit-eating grin on her face.

"I've decided I want you to fire me today and not hire me back until next Monday. I'm going up to the North Shore for a few days of R & R."

"Nope, you're needed right here. And I don't see any broken bones."

"Is that all it would take? I'll go back to my desk and slam my hand in a drawer. Really."

"Courtney, how could you do that to me? Out me before I'm ready? You should be ashamed of yourself."

"But I'm not. I'm in charge of your communications. I communicated; no more, no less."

"I'm going home for the day, I think."

"Can't. That's why I came in. I just got an email. We need to have the Wexler account updated by the close of business tomorrow, and you're going to be with Kathleen tomorrow. We'd better get busy on it now, if you want to be out of here by six."

Sigh.

❊ ❊ ❊

I got up and made breakfast, then worked from the office at home for a couple hours. Minnie was there looking after Kathleen, enjoyably listening to her music while still getting Kathleen whatever she needed. She kept the music turned down to a level where she could easily hear her patient, unlike Kathleen when she was jamming to the tunes. I got up around eleven thirty and cooked some chicken breasts to go into a chef's salad for the three of us at noon. We all ate in the living room, Kathleen well able to feed herself from her table.

"I'm going to go do something you can't do," I musically intoned to Kathleen.

"What's that?" she asked.

"I'm going to go take a hot shower!"

"You stone cold bitch!" she laughed at me.

"Look, when you have all your hardware off and you can climb the steps on your own, then you can take a shower. Until then, you'll just have to let me do what I did the other day."

"Everything you did?"

"If you want," I grinned at her.

"Oh, that'd be very, very nice," she purred at me.

Finally, it was time to get ready to go. I brought her underwear for the trip, as well as socks and a pair of sneakers. I took off her top and bottom one at a time to get her underwear on, then put them back on. Then I pulled her socks on and laced her sneakers. Precisely at one, the doorbell rang. A burly man was pushing a wheelchair. I wondered how he was going to get Kathleen down the steps without a ramp, but he used sheer muscle power, rolling her slowly down, one step at a time and holding her chair, keeping her from slamming down to the next step. The mobility van had an electric lift gate for the wheelchair and a place to secure it in the back end, while I entered the front end then found a seat next to Kathleen near the back. Apparently, we were the only passengers for this run today.

At the hospital, we went to orthopedics and only had to wait about thirty minutes.

"Hi, I'm Dr. Stuermer. I'm going to be taking your gear off today. We're going to be numbing you up with many shots from the elbow down. Just local anesthetics, so there hopefully won't be too much pain. What you will feel is a *lot* of tugging and pulling. It might be a little scary, but it's nothing to worry about. You're already taking hydrocodone for pain, right?"

"Yes. Some. Not the full amount, just when I need it," Kathleen replied.

"For forty-eight hours after this comes off, you take two every six hours whether you think you need them or not. Once the pain is there it's hard to overcome. If you need more, let me know, and I'll give you a new prescription. In addition, I'm giving you two OxyContin: take one this afternoon and one in the morning. Again, take them whether you think you need them or not. They may knock you out. If so, good. You'll sleep through it. You know how a doctor gives you a shot and says this will just be a little pinch or sting? Well, I'll tell you the honest truth. Most of my patients tell me that the pain is unbearable for a few days, I'm just saying. You may not think so, but I want to be up front with you to prepare you, just in case."

"We appreciate that, doctor," I said on Kathleen's behalf.

Including time to numb her arm up, it took just over an hour to get the halo off. Then, he made Kathleen move her hand to test for range of motion and to see if there were any kinks, which there were none. He had her squeeze his hand. He was totally amazed that after being in the halo for nearly three months she could nearly cut off his circulation. Everybody underestimates my li'l firefighter! I had to fight to keep from laughing in his face. Finally, it was time to go, and we took the mobility bus home, then got Kathleen back in her bed. We'd gotten the first OxyContin down her throat at the hospital, and she was practically on Mars. I'm surprised she didn't turn her head sideways with her tongue lolling out like a dog in summer. I don't see how some people eat them like candy for recreational use!

"Minnie, she's going to be asleep until later tonight and then, I'm home. Go ahead and go home early today."

"Okay, I'll do it just this once. I'll go home and bake some cookies for my grandson's class, I think. That'll make the kids all happy. I'll see you both tomorrow, bright and early."

I knew how Kathleen was about being clean all the time, so, I manhandled her, got her clothes off, then gave her another sponge bath. After I was done, I got a clean pair of shorts and tee shirt on her. It took all my strength. Just lying there passed out, she was pure dead weight and disconnected. I worked and struggled so hard trying to get Kathleen cleaned up and dressed that I was sweating. I went up to take a shower. While I was in, I thought I heard something, but figured it was my imagination. When I turned off the water, I heard it again. It was Kathleen's bell.

"Just a minute, baby. I'm all wet. Let me dry off, and I'll be right down," I yelled.

"Okay," she yelled back up.

I toweled off briefly, wrapped my hair in a towel, and pulled my robe on. Walking down the stairs, I heard a strange percussive sound. As I was nearing the bottom of the stairs, I could see Kathleen slowly clapping her hands together.

"I bet you think you're clever, don't you?" I asked.

"Look what I can do," she said as she continued to do it a couple dozen more times.

"Okay, I get it. You have both of your hands back."

"Want me to make love to you?"

"Do you want to?"

"Actually, I want to eat and go back to sleep. This medicine is kicking my ass! Hey! These are different clothes! What happened to my clothes? And my bra is off!"

"So's your underwear, actually. I stripped you, gave you a sponge bath, and got you new clothes."

"How did I not wake up?"

"The magic of modern chemicals. Let me go make dinner."

"Just make sandwiches. I'm not that hungry. And before you do that, would you come lie down with me for a few minutes?"

"Sure, baby."

"Get on the correct side though. You can, now that my arm is freed up."

In our bed upstairs, she lies down on the right side of the bed and I get the left side, with her left arm over me. So that's how I got in tonight for the first time since she'd been home. And it took all of two minutes for her to fall soundly asleep again. I slipped out from under her arm, made the sandwiches, poured some tea, and returned to her with them.

"Hey, stinky. Wake up. You need to eat...."

"Hmm?"

"Wake up and eat. Aren't you glad that Dr. Stuermer said you didn't need your mask except for sleeping now? That should make you happy."

"Mm-hmm. Mphf."

"Come on, let's eat," I said, raising the back of the bed. By the time it was raised fully, her eyes finally began fluttering open.

She fell asleep three times while eating, and once she finished, I made her go to the bathroom before going back to bed. I also made her take the hydrocodone as directed. She wasn't awake when her head hit the pillow. I put the head of the bed back down flat and covered her up, put the dishes in the sink, and went to bed with the four cats; Tinkerbelle and Ivan plus the two kittens I had gotten from the new litter, Ellen and Moe.

※ ※ ※

"Nancy, is there a reason that you're the only one in the whole family that hasn't so much as acknowledged me? I mean, I know we were never that close growing up, but don't you think we're a little past that now? I've sent you several emails and texts, and you haven't answered a single one of them," I said exasperatedly.

"It's not lot like you make time for us. I mean, you are the ones that haven't had children up until now, and you've not made a single trip back to Houston to see anybody."

"That's because Kathleen moved to Medic 4 and was the new person on the team, so she had to work the holidays. Then, she moved to the LifeFlight crew here in town. Again, none of the crews got off for holidays because that's their busiest time. Then, she got on with the Highway Patrol. Once more, the holidays were the busy times. We kept meaning to do it, but the timing was all wrong. Now, I'm already at the point where I've used up a lot of time off with Kathleen's hospitalization, and I'll be taking off six weeks of maternity leave or more. Hopefully, toward the end of that, if the baby is old enough to travel and Kathleen is still on disability, we'll come back for a week. Jesus, you're actually being sort of a bitch about this, to tell you the truth."

"Is there anything else you wanted?"

"No, I just thought you might be a little bit happy about your nephew is all. Forgive me for bothering you," I said curtly as I clicked off the phone.

Truth be told, I still loved Nancy, but I didn't care for her much. Not at all. She was the single most self-centered person I think I'd ever met. I walked out of the office into the living room and was plenty surly.

"Why so glum, chum?" asked Kathleen.

"One word: Nancy."

"Enough said."

"How did physical therapy go today? Day five, so you should be getting a little used to it," I said.

"I begged her to double the weights they strap on, but she wasn't having any part of it. I told her that if they didn't increase the weights next week I'd do it myself. She wasn't too happy with my attitude, but she's happy that I'm working hard. She told me I push harder than most of her patients, and I reminded her that I'm used to working out and that's why I want to increase the weights. She just kept saying, 'Not yet.' It's frustrating."

Kathleen had therapy Monday, Wednesday, and Friday. Thus far, she'd been doing it for almost two weeks. I got home on Thursday afternoon of her second week after Miss Minnie had gone for the day, and Kathleen wasn't in her bed. I looked around the screen and she wasn't on the toilet. Suddenly, my throat constricted, and I panicked. I ran to the back of the hallway and down the stairs, fearing that somehow, she'd gotten up and fallen down the stairs, but she wasn't there. My mind was racing into overtime. I rushed back up the stairs and around into the kitchen thinking maybe I'd missed her, but she wasn't there. I took the stairs up two at a time, dodging the four cats that were coming down to greet me. It was then, I heard the noise. The shower was running. I darted into the bathroom and flung the shower curtain open, getting water all over the floor. Kathleen was washing her hair.

"*Kathleen Marie Pope! What in the hell do you think you're doing!*" I screamed at the top of my lungs.

She jumped a little at having been scared but continued to wash her hair.

"Shut the curtain. You're causing a cold breeze," she told me matter-of-factly.

I quickly stripped down and got in the back of the shower to help her.

"Hold on to the shower rod, but make sure you don't pull it down."

She did as she was told, and I finished washing her hair, then applied cream rinse.

"Have you soaped up yet?" I inquired.

"Nope."

I grabbed a washrag, soaped it up generously, and began to wash her from head to toe. When I was done, I took the hand-held shower head and rinsed her down, so she was squeaky clean. I turned the water off and reached out to get a towel, dabbing her dry while she was still in the shower. I opened the curtain and held both her hands while she stepped out of the shower.

"Now, lean against the counter," I commanded.

"I'm fine."

"If you know what's good for you, I suggest you keep your mouth shut!" I snapped as I glared at her icily.

She did as she was told while I snatched up a second towel and dried myself.

"Wait here."

I went into our bedroom and got some clean pajamas, dressing us both.

"May I say something?" begged Kathleen.

"What?" I asked, still snapping and glaring.

"Did you or did you not say when my hardware was off and when I could get up the stairs I could have a nice hot shower?"

I breathed a huge sigh and dropped my shoulders. She'd been home exactly two weeks and was doing what they expected she might be doing in six to eight weeks. My baby was an amazing woman. I got under Kathleen's right arm to support her, and instead of going downstairs, I walked her into our bedroom and pulled down the blanket and sheet. She crawled in and practically purred at the comfort. For dinner that night I made a breakfast and brought it up to the bedroom. For the first time in four months, I slept in our bed with my wife, something that at one time I wondered if I would ever be able to do again. Thinking about it, I started crying.

"Why are you crying?" asked Kathleen.

"Because I love you so much, and I thought that I had lost you."

Just as I was dozing off that night, I felt Kathleen's now unfettered left hand slip beneath the band of my pajama bottoms. She began tracing her fingers back and forth in the hair at the juncture of my thighs.

"Stop."

"Why?"

"I'm not in the mood," I said.

Kathleen reached up behind me and shoved her right arm underneath my neck, then started nibbling below my right ear, seductively, slowly.

"Stop that! It tickles," I told her.

'You mean this?" as she continued working her way down my neck.

Sigh.

"Play with my butt, will you?" I pleaded, rolling over on my stomach.

FURTHER INTO FIRE

Kathleen pulled the sheet and blanket back and began tugging at my pajama shorts, pulling them down over my hips as I raised up, then down my legs as I put my legs in the air slightly. She got behind me, sitting on my calves and began to knead and massage my derriere, relaxing me, yet at the same time exciting me, causing me to become wet with anticipation. She occasionally leaned down and kissed my bottom, letting her tongue make little circular patterns on me. Finally, she gave me one long tongue swipe from front to back, completely furrowed, and I came unglued. We made love half the night. Kathleen, my old Kathleen, was back in my life.

"You know, in the morning you'll have to be back downstairs in your bed before Miss Minnie comes, don't you?" I quipped.

"Yeah, I figured as much. Grab my pajamas off the floor for me, would you, so we can finally get a little bit of sleep before we have to get up?"

"Nope," I said with a mischievous grin on my face, only pulling the sheet up over us and settling into Kathleen's body with us both still nude.

"Good night, sweetie."

"Good night, baby. You know that I love you more than life itself, don't you?" I put to her.

"Me too. Me too."

Being a Friday, I wanted so badly to call in sick. There wasn't a lot going on. After quickly checking my calendar, I decided instead to call Courtney and tell her I was working from home today. I fixed breakfast at seven thirty, but at eight o'clock, I called a builder that Pop uses.

"Pete Birkhead."

"Hey, Pete. Bella Pope here, Kevin's daughter-in-law. I need something done, and I need a total rush on it. Simple, but important. I thought of you first, but if you can't do it, maybe you can recommend somebody that can."

"Well, I'll try. Whatcha got?" he asked.

"I need a second railing on two stairwells. Straight shot. One's twenty-three feet, and the other is nineteen feet. I need them to be rock solid. They can even be the handicap access kind in brushed steel if you think that's best. I need it for Kathleen to use both hands to get up and down the steps while she's convalescing. I don't know if we'll keep it afterwards or not, but we need it for the next few months. Money's not so much an object, but time's critical. Can you do it?"

"Actually, I have a couple of free days while we wait on supplies for a really big job I'm on. Let me come over this morning. I'll look at it and get started. What's your address?"

"I'll text it to you. I'll be working from home today, so I'll be here. See you later."

Minnie showed up at nine o'clock sharp, and within five minutes of her arrival, Pete showed up with his work belt including a protractor and laser level. He laid out the lines on the wall, then he came to talk to me.

"I like your idea of using the handicap accessory bars. They'll support a helluva lot more weight, and when you don't need them anymore we can take them down. Leave the board up that I'm installing as the main support and simply put plugs in the attachment points. It'll look really nice, I think."

"How much is this going to set me back?"

"Both stairs? Two thousand. I can go with wooden railings instead, but that will still cost you around twelve hundred and will not be anywhere near as good."

"No, go for the handicapped railing. And one more thing. Would you put a grab bar in the shower upstairs as well?"

"Sure, no problem."

"When can you be done?"

"Assuming I get all the parts this morning, I can get the upstairs rail and the bathroom done today. I'll go ahead and take off now and go to the yard. Back in a bit."

"Pete, thank you so much for handling this for us."

"No problem. Glad to help."

"I take it from what I could hear you're having a second rail put up the stairs?" asked Kathleen.

"And down the stairs as well. As you get better, you'll also be able to go down and work out without falling, do laundry again, things like that, and I won't have to worry."

"Sounds good."

I stayed out of the way until lunch when I fixed us some homemade chicken soup, then went back into the home office until after the physical therapist was done. The occupational therapist wouldn't be coming back for two weeks until there were more things to do. At about four o'clock, Minnie made her way home for the day, and Pete was only about fifteen minutes behind. He had indeed completed the upstairs stairwell and the shower. It was just me and Kathleen now. I was still working, however, and Kathleen was lying in her hospital bed listening to music. The doorbell rang. I wondered who it could be at this time of day. I opened the door and got the surprise of my life. The girl standing in the door was crying, her mascara had been running, her face was puffy, her eyes looked like she'd been cutting an onion, and her shoulders were completely slumped.

"May I…May I…come…" she stammered away.

"Melanie, come in," I welcomed her with a flourish of my arm.

It was Kathleen's ex-girlfriend—the one that had sent her into a dark tailspin for over five years when they split up, and the one she'd found making out with somebody else at a Halloween party those years ago. As soon as she was standing inside the living room, she practically had a mental breakdown. Not only did she begin to bawl her head off with uncontrollable, body-wrenching sobs, but she fell to the floor. I ran to her, helped her up, and got her to the couch where she didn't slow down, but curled up in a fetal ball, rocking herself.

I ran into the kitchen and poured her a small brandy, hoping that would help, but when she smelled it, she knocked it out of my hand.

"Okay, you don't have to have any. I just thought it would help."

I went back to the kitchen, put the glass in the sink, and got a cool, wet washrag. I walked back over to the couch, scooted her back a few inches, sat on the edge myself, and began to wipe down her face. I wiped her forehead and her face to clean her up and cool her off. After about thirty minutes, she was sound asleep. After she fell asleep and you could see the rise and fall of her small shoulders, I went and sat on the bed with Kathleen.

"What do you suppose all that is about?" I asked Kathleen.

"I have absolutely no idea. Are you going to have her arrested?" she giggled.

"I think perhaps not. At least, not until we find out what's going on," I ventured.

I fixed onion burgers for dinner along with baked beans. Kathleen wanted to eat at the kitchen table. I figured if she could shower by herself after crawling up the stairs, why not. I made her use her walker just the same and was surprised when she didn't give me a fight at all. After she was seated, I went into the living room to wake Melanie up. It took some doing. I figured she was totally tired, but I got her up and sitting at the table. I think she was surprised we brought her to the table. She had a totally astounded look on her face as we all held hands around the table and I said a prayer out loud, giving thanks not only for the food but for the friends that had been brought to our table. We ate in silence until each of us were sated.

"So, Melanie. You look like you're in trouble. What's going on, and why did you come to us?" I started the inquisition.

Her head hung low and her eyes were averted, as they had been since she'd walked in the door.

"You're right. I am in trouble, and I just don't know where to turn. My Uncle Dalton was my last living relative, other than my Aunt

Kathryn. Dalton loved me, in spite of who and what I am. Kathryn is a complete homophobe though, and a real self-centered, money-hungry bitch. Dalton had a million-dollar life insurance policy, and we're both listed as beneficiaries. But in the last year I've been hospitalized twice for severe depression, so Kathryn is trying to have me committed against my will, have herself made the executrix of my estate, and make it so she can spend the money any way she sees fit. I have an old friend from high school that works for the county, and she called me and warned me. I left my apartment with the clothes on my back. I'm sorry, but I didn't know where else to turn…" she said, breaking down again.

"Melanie, listen to me. Stop that! I have an entire team of lawyers that work with me. You're going to stay in our guest bedroom until Monday. Let me talk to them, and we'll see about getting an injunction and getting this whole mess cleaned up," I rebuffed her.

"But I don't have any money. I had to just skip out!"

"You won't need any for now. Do you have a job?" I queried.

"Brenda's Café," she nodded her head.

"I'll call them and tell them you've got a medical emergency, and you won't be back for a week."

"I need to call AnnaMaria too. She'll worry. She doesn't sleep if she doesn't know where I am. She doesn't even sleep if she does know but I'm not in bed with her."

"That's your roommate? Your partner?" I asked her.

Once again, she hung her head down, but managed to nod.

"Does she know what's happening?" I questioned.

"Yeah, but then I just took off. Look, I'm sorry to have come here. I know you two don't like me. I should leave–"

"No, just sit down. We'll work through this together. We're not monsters, Melanie. Come here."

I picked up my cell phone and dialed the two-digit code to make it an unknown call, then handed the phone to Melanie.

"Call her now. The number won't be traceable by anybody else listening. Dial the number and give it back to me."

She did so. Finally, AnnaMaria picked up after about the sixth ring.

"H-h-hello?" she managed in a staccato.

"AnnaMaria? My name is Bella Pope. You don't know me, but perhaps you've heard of my wife, Kathleen Pope?"

"Uh, yes."

"Well, Melanie is very confused and very hurt, and she is apparently the victim of a witch hunt right now because of that lying and conniving aunt of hers, Kathryn. She wasn't sure where to go, and she turned up at our doorstep a few hours ago. She took a long nap, then we fed her dinner. I'm going to have a couple of lawyers work on her case first thing Monday morning, but in the meanwhile, I think it's important that she lay low, so she can't get picked up. And I think that means no communications. But I wanted to let you know that everything's all right. Okay, hon?"

"You're going to help her?" AnnaMaria said as I heard her starting to cry.

"Do you work at the same restaurant as Melanie?" I asked further.

"Yes."

"I've already told them she has a medical emergency and won't be in for a week. Do they know you two are girlfriends?"

"No, just roommates."

"Okay, when they ask, tell them she has a swollen ovary and has to be on total bed rest and is at a friend's house. If they ask where, tell them you aren't certain. Got it?"

"Got it."

"Now, knowing she's safe and sound, you need to get some rest. She's going to be just fine." I tried to be positive, giving her some support.

"I'll try," AnnaMaria whimpered, hanging up the phone.

"Now, Melanie, make sure you don't contact AnnaMaria with your phone, so they can't trace where you are for the next week or so. Okay? You'll take the guest bedroom upstairs," I said.

Melanie sat there almost in a trance-like state. She'd come to our house not knowing where else to go, but never fully expecting to get any help from us; she'd come out of sheer desperation. Now, here we were essentially lending aid and comfort to the enemy. It had her baffled. I went upstairs to our bedroom and pulled out a pair of smaller sweats that she could tighten by the cords, petite as she was. I gave them to her, inviting her to go take a shower.

"I'll take the clothes you have on now and wash them for you. Okay?" I prompted.

Melanie numbly nodded. I'd never noticed before what a pixie she really was. The sweats were so baggy they nearly swallowed her up. By seven thirty, she was upstairs in bed and out like a light.

"You know, for all the talk about me being a hero all the time, you sure came through tonight, Bella."

"Well, when somebody is truly in trouble, I think all of us would like to help as best we can. I just can't believe that a woman that's already going to get five hundred thousand dollars is going to try and have her niece committed to an institution, so she can get control of twice that amount of money. It stymies me."

When I left for work in the morning, Melanie hadn't stirred an inch. I'd been tempted to wake her for breakfast, but we had cereal and instant oatmeal, if she wanted something later.

"Guess who showed up at our house last night?" I asked Courtney.

"The Brothers Grimm?" she snorted.

"Melanie, Kathleen's ex."

"You mean the one who showed up at the hospital?"

"The very same."

"Why, on God's green earth?" she asked, her mouth agape.

I gave her the thirty second version of the story. Courtney just shook her head.

"It just goes to show, no matter what goes wrong in your life, somebody else always has it worse. So, what are you going to do about it?" she wondered.

"I'm going to call and see if there's something we can do to get her out of this jam. She's got a girlfriend and everything right now. She's only about twenty-five, and she's running scared."

I picked up the phone and dialed a number.

"Legal. This is Penny."

"Hey, Penny. This is Bella Pope from Accounting, Region Three. Is Celeste or Randy there?"

"I know Celeste is; she just walked in. Wait just a sec…" she said, putting me on hold.

"Celeste Wannamaker. How may I help you?"

"Celeste, Bella."

"Oh, hi, Bella. Long time no see. How are you doing?"

"Don't sound so happy to see me until you find out what I want."

"Oh? Sounds ominous…."

I described the situation briefly and told her we were hiding Melanie out at our house for the time being. I asked her if she would mind coming by tomorrow to talk to Melanie and see if she thought there was anything she could do to help. She agreed and said she'd be by about ten o'clock after she dropped her son off for little league practice. I thanked her and hung up. Maybe there was hope after all; she sounded pretty upbeat. I called Courtney in, and we began wading through the work for the day.

When I got home, Bella was in the hospital bed, and Melanie was curled up on the couch in the fetal position, sound asleep with tear streaks running down her cheeks. She was anything but the tough girl that was on our front porch three years ago looking for Kathleen. Life had mellowed this girl. I leaned down and kissed Kathleen deeply.

"She's nothing like the hurt, angry kid who showed up on our doorstep before we got married," I said.

"I know. It's like she's a totally different person than I've ever known. She's been awake part of the day, and we've talked. Remember when she knocked the brandy from your hand? She used to be Miss Party Girl, USA. After I caught her with the other girl at Halloween, she later realized it was because she was totally drunk. She doesn't drink any alcohol now. She spent over half an hour apologizing to me for breaking my heart, her own words, and she was crying the whole time. I told her I've moved on, and I'm happy. I asked her if she was happy with AnnaMaria, and she smiled for the first time since being here. I think she's madly in love with her. And I'm glad for her."

"Wait just a minute...."

I picked my phone up from my purse. I flipped back through recently called numbers and called Brenda's Café.

"Hello, is AnnaMaria working this evening?"

"Yes, one minute. Uh, she's at a table. Can you hold?"

"Yes, that would be wonderful."

It took about three minutes for her to pick up the phone.

"This is AnnaMaria. Who is this?"

"AnnaMaria, this is Bella Pope again. What time do you get off tonight?"

"At eight o'clock. It'll be about a quarter after eight when I actually get done. Why?"

"There could be people watching your apartment. I'm going to pick you up directly from work. There are clothes here at my apartment you can wear, sweats, just like we have Melanie wearing. Do you work tomorrow?"

"No, I'm off until Tuesday."

"Good. Do you have anything else you have to do?"

"No."

"Do you have a pet to feed?"

"We have a cat."

"Do you have a friend you can call?"

"Um, sure."

"Good. You can call them from here either later tonight or in the morning. I'll see you in a couple of hours. Okay?"

"Okay. But can I ask you a question?"

"Sure. Shoot."

"Why are you doing this? I mean, I know about the history between Melanie and Kathleen, and it didn't end very well."

"Don't you worry about that, hon. You just worry about getting over here and holding your sweet girlfriend and making sure she gets better. She's in pretty rough shape. Right now, she feels totally abandoned and attacked, and without you she's pretty lonely."

"I'll see you when you get here then."

I went back in the living room and sat in the chair by the bed.

"Want lasagna?"

"Mmm. Sure. Hey! Are you fixing it for me or your new girlfriend?"

"Why, my beautiful wife, of course."

I leaned in over the bed.

"I'll even make love to you tonight, if you'll promise to keep the noise down," I thought I whispered.

"I heard that," laughed Melanie.

Apparently not.

The three of us laughed long and hard.

"Hey, girl, it's all right. We're married!" I shouted.

"It's okay, I don't care," she said, but her eyes clouded over immediately just the same.

"Hey, kid. Cheer up. I have a surprise for you later tonight. A good one."

"What kind of surprise?"

"I just told you, a good one."

"Okay," she said, her eyes closing once again, snuggling down into the couch.

Forty-five minutes later, I shook Melanie gently to wake her. Kathleen was already at the table, three iced tea glasses were poured, and three steaming plates of lasagna were ready to be devoured. Tonight, unlike last night, Melanie tore a pretty large hole in her plate, although still not finishing all her food. I cleared the table and cut up an apple for Kathleen. After that, I glanced at my watch. It was ten minutes to eight. I quietly slipped on some shoes, grabbed my purse, and walked out the front door without saying a word.

"Where is Bella going?" asked Melanie.

"Beats the crap out of me. She's pretty independent. She usually tells me where, but if she said there was a surprise involved, I'll be as completely in the dark as you until the unveiling," sighed Kathleen.

I walked in the door at eight thirty-five, without pulling it shut behind me.

"Here's your surprise, Melanie," I exclaimed jubilantly, jumping with one foot forward, holding my hands out in front of me.

"What is it?"

Timidly, AnnaMaria peeked her head around the door frame, slowly walking into the living room.

"*AnnaMaria!*" she yelled, hurtling up off the couch, running across the room, and jumping into the waiting arms of her lover.

Both the girls started to cry very hard.

"Hey, I thought this would make you happy," I joked with her.

"Oh, I'm *so* happy. I'm happy like you wouldn't believe."

Melanie stepped back to look in AnnaMaria's eyes, still not believing I brought her here.

"AnnaMaria, you can bunk down on the couch while you're here," I said, hardly able to suppress a smile.

"All right," she said a little dejectedly.

"Hey, I'm just kidding. Of course, you can sleep with Melanie in the guest bedroom. I'm not a witch, I know you two are girlfriends."

Her smile lit up like a Christmas tree with ten strings of lights on it.

We all stayed downstairs and talked for about an hour: about the batshit-crazy aunt, about the sorrow of losing Uncle Dalton, about the diner, about their cat, about our cats as the girls played with the four of them, about how they met, about how they were planning on the day they could save up a little more money and eventually get married themselves, and about the fact that AnnaMaria had grown up in foster care as an orphan.

"Well, look, kiddos, the old lady and I are going upstairs and watch a movie. Anything you want in the kitchen is fine. There's popcorn in the far-right cabinet. There's cereal in the pantry. Oh, before I forget, AnnaMaria, let me get you some sweats like Melanie. You can sleep in them and wear them around here until your clothes get washed. If it weren't dangerous to go by your apartment, I would have picked you up some clothes. I just didn't think it was a good idea."

"Oh, I agree. I'll come up with you," she said.

"I will too. I'm pretty tired," said Melanie.

Kathleen had already started her climb up the stairs, so we had to wait for her to power herself up, on her arms for the most part as her legs were still pretty weak. I went into the kitchen in the meanwhile and got two large, plastic tumblers and filled them with ice, taking one for me and Kathleen and giving one to the girls.

"Oh, thank you. Thank you very much," said AnnaMaria.

I dug in the dresser, got out another pair of sweats, and gave them to her.

"After you have these on, go downstairs to the basement and put the clothes you're wearing now into the basket on the washing machine. I'll run them through in the morning, so at least you'll have underwear again…unless you're comfy without."

"Oh, there's no hurry. I'll be comfy in just the sweats. And at home I never wear a bra, so it's no big deal," said AnnaMaria.

"When you come back up, turn out all the lights. And make sure the bathroom door stays open when you're not in it. That's where the cat box is."

"Will do! Hey, Bella?" asked Melanie.

"Yeah?"

"Thank you so much!"

Both girls rushed me and hugged me so tightly I could barely breathe.

"You know, Kathleen, it's possible that the little girl who once broke your heart may end up being your lifelong friend."

"Funny. I was just thinking that."

"One thing you never told me about Melanie…"

"What's that?"

"You were a fucking cradle robber!"

Don't give me that shit, you knew that before we got married, you twit!

Kathleen said nothing but had a wide grin on her face. I heard a lot of giggling coming from the guest bedroom. I held my index finger up to my lips, smiling. I crept out into the hallway and banged on their door.

"AnnaMaria, if you don't stop this all-night giggle fest, I won't ever let you come back for a sleepover. Do you hear me?" I said, stifling a laugh.

"Why don't you go and make love to your wife and try to keep the noise down!" Melanie yelled back, a cacophony of giggles emanating from the room.

"Nighty night, girls."

"Good night, Mrs. Pope," they sang back in unison.

"I hope Celeste has good news for us when she comes over tomorrow morning," I told Kathleen as I slid beneath the sheets.

"Forget tomorrow. If I promise not to make loud noises, you promised to make love to me."

So, I did.

※ ※ ※

The following morning found me sitting in the chair in the living room with my feet up on the bed, cradling a glass of iced tea. Kathleen was pulling her feet up into the lotus position, trying to work some limberness back into her legs by stretching. Melanie and AnnaMaria were sitting on the couch, heads leaned into each other, arms intertwined.

It was about twenty-five after ten when Celeste showed up.

"Sorry I'm late. There was another soccer mom that wouldn't shut up. I was about at my breaking point. As much as I try and restrain my potty mouth when I'm in polite society, I was on the verge of asking her if she wanted to go play 'hide-and-go-fuck-yourself.'"

Everybody in the room had a laugh at that one. Celeste moved over to the couch by the girls and pulled out a pad.

"I've done a little research already. I've looked into your situation, and I have a few questions for you up front. How do you pay for your rent and bills?"

"We pool our money, sharing, but Melanie always writes the checks. Mostly out of habit because she was already there when I moved in with her," answered AnnaMaria quickly.

"When were you in the hospital and for how long?"

"Last year, twice. The first time was for about two weeks. The second time was for about ten days. The first stay was to put me on medication and observe me while they found out what medications would work. The second stay was to adjust my medications a bit," answered Melanie.

"Were you suicidal?"

"Well, not really. I didn't want to hurt myself, I just didn't want to be alive, if that makes sense."

"But you didn't try and harm yourself."

"No. Never."

"That's good. I assume they were voluntary committals, then? Both times?"

"Yes, certainly."

"Well, I think I have all I need. You've got nothing to worry about. You've supported yourself, and you've never been a threat to yourself or anybody else. What I do need you to do, though, is sign this. Then I can retrieve your bank records to show the court you've paid everything yourself. I should be able to go to the courts Monday and have everything rescinded. That is, if the bitch has already filed. I'll also file a restraining order against her. I'm also going before the probate court and will file to make sure she can't do anything screwy there."

"Um, how much is this going to cost me?" asked Melanie.

"Oh, no, child. This isn't going to cost you anything. This is going to come out of the pocket of one Kathryn Stevenson. Trust me. And I'm going to enjoy every minute of it."

"Are you sure?"

"Don't you worry about a thing! You just hang out here for the next week and let me handle it…if that's all right with Kathleen and Bella?" she said, looking our way.

"Oh, I've already told you it's fine," I replied.

"Well, I've got to go. Practice will almost be over, and today is my day to take everybody to Dairy Queen for ice cream. Toodles, ladies."

I had to take AnnaMaria back on Monday night, so she could work an opening shift on Tuesday, but she and Melanie were happy as two kittens in a litter sucking on their momma's teats now that things were turning around. I got a call in my office on Thursday. Celeste was calling from the probate courthouse. She had filed for a change in the will, providing proof that Kathryn had tried to have Melanie committed, have herself installed as the executrix, and was suing to get the entire estate. She didn't know if it would fly or not, but she was going to give it a try. It brought a huge smile to my face. When I took Melanie back to her apartment on Saturday morning, she cried. Not just a little bit, but a complete deluge.

"What's the matter with you now, funny face? Things are going to be okay."

"I just don't understand why you and Kathleen are doing all of this for me, especially after what I did to her."

"Look, we believe that everybody gets a second chance in life. And you've turned out to be a very sweet, genuine person, as we've seen over the last week, and we're proud to call you our friend. And AnnaMaria too. Now, come here and give me a hug, you."

We hugged each other for over five minutes, and finally, Melanie stopped crying. My shirt was wet from her tears, but it was a small price to pay, and I genuinely felt good.

When I got home I didn't see Kathleen, so I assumed she was upstairs. When I didn't find her up there, I went downstairs and looked in the kitchen and the office but didn't see her anywhere. Then, I heard a barely perceptible noise emanating from the basement. I walked downstairs and could hardly believe my eyes. Even though she was bracing solidly with her arms, Kathleen was on the treadmill, walking a slow but deliberate pace.

I walked over to her and crossed my arms over my chest, rocked back on my left leg, and began to tap my right toe sharply on the concrete.

"Hi."

"A-hem!"

"I'll be done in about twenty minutes."

"You know, there are times that you don't make me very happy. You know that, don't you?" I hammered out in staccato

"Yeah, well, I'm sure you'll get over it…or not."

I reached over and turned off the motor, and it gradually came to a halt. I reached over and gave Kathleen a deep and meaningful kiss.

FURTHER INTO FIRE

"Why do you always have to be the tough girl? My tough girl!"
She laughed.
"I thought you liked it?"
"I do! In fact, I love it!" I answered back.

I reached over and turned the motor back on, then went over to the washing machine and put in a load of laundry. I left Kathleen in the basement to do her workout. When I hadn't seen her in over half an hour, I began to wonder. When I heard the washing machine buzz, I went downstairs to put the clothes into the dryer. She was sitting on the bench lifting weights. Argh! My Kathleen! Well, it was what saved her life, after all. It was what she was made of.

❦ ❦ ❦

I hated maternity clothes. Mostly because they looked like…well…maternity clothes, not the least bit flattering. 'Hey! Fat lady here!' What I did like, though, was being pregnant. I loved it, at least thus far. At four months I only stuck out about an inch and a half. It worried me. I thought something might be wrong. At four months and one week, though, I stuck out about three inches. What happened in that week was anybody's guess. I mushroomed almost overnight. At just short of six months, I looked like I was carrying a soccer ball underneath my shirt, hence the maternity clothes. How I longed for a pair of jeans again.

Kathleen was forever standing behind me, her hands softly caressing little Kevin. I loved that too; it always comforted me. Never once did I tell her to stop. It somehow made her more connected to me…to us. It was, after all, her baby too.

Thanksgiving was in two weeks. It was all set for Pops' house, as usual, but I told him it would be a plus four instead. He didn't question it. He said it was no problem, and he'd tell Martha to make sure there was enough food. I tried to tell him we didn't need any extra food since there was so much left over at a normal Thanksgiving, and he laughed at that.

Melanie and AnnaMaria came over to our house at about ten thirty or so to make sure they were early enough.

"Why don't you girls take off your coats and mittens and get comfortable? We won't be going over for about thirty to forty-five minutes anyway," I prompted them.

They took them off and stacked them on one end of the couch, then they both sat upright with their hands folded one over the other, their left hands on top, grinning, and not saying a thing.

"Okay, what's up? I know there's something," I began questioning them, and then, I noticed their hands.

"Oh, my God! Are you kidding me?"

Both of them wore matching solitaire engagement rings. I rushed over to them, grabbing their hands, and holding them up together.

"When did this happen?" I asked, excitedly.

"Last weekend. On Friday, we got our settlement from the court. We were afraid it was going to be held up for a year or so. Normally, it takes well over a year, but once Celeste filed the suit and the judge found out what Aunt Kathryn had done, he wouldn't have any part of it. Her lawyer kept trying to get extensions, but he told them flat out 'no' and said it was the most despicable thing he'd ever seen. Can you imagine? In only two months. And, you'll never believe it!" exclaimed an exuberant Melanie.

"Believe what?" I asked, so happy for the two of them.

"He awarded me seven hundred fifty thousand dollars! Plus, Aunt Kathryn has to pay Celeste's and the court's fees of one hundred thousand out of her share. She only has one hundred fifty thousand dollars left! Serves that cold-hearted bitch right. And the case was closed with prejudice, so she can never reopen it!"

"Oh, I'm so happy for you! What are you going to do with all that money? You need to be careful. Do not go out and spend it all!"

"Oh, no. We're not. We're going to continue to work until January, and then, we'll quit. We're going to go to school full-time, and we're both going to get our RN licenses. How cool is that?"

"Sounds like a cool, level-headed decision to me!" shouted Kathleen out of pure joy.

"Um, Kathleen?" Melanie asked quietly.

"Yes?"

"I'm so sorry for the way I was to you. Not just that night, but overall. I wish I had acted then like I am now, I mean like the true me. I think I was always a coward, and I tried to cover it up by pretending to be something I wasn't. I seriously want to apologize to you for my actions."

"Melanie, you've got to get over this. I can see how you are. I can see how you've grown. It's like, the hospital bed is gone now, so that part of my life is over. You've got to put it behind you. I'm not a super-duper religious person, but I know that God will always forgive you, so you've got to forgive yourself. You must see that the four of us have gotten really close over the last couple of months. That alone should show you that I don't harbor any ill will toward you, honey. Okay?"

FURTHER INTO FIRE

"Okay," she managed to mumble with a slight grin, leaning into AnnaMaria.

Both of them looked down at their rings and smiled. I got it. It was the same thing that Kathleen and I did with each other when we first got our rings...and sometimes still did.

"You're getting huge," AnnaMaria said to me.

"And you've got a big mouth on you!"

Everybody laughed.

Finally, we got to Pops' house and made our way up onto the porch. We knocked, and he came to the door. One at a time, he welcomed us and gave us a big hug. When he saw Melanie, his eyes bugged out.

"Melanie?"

"Hi, Pops. Oh, I've missed you," she said, giving him a bear hug.

Pops didn't know what to say; he was confused.

"Hiya, Pops. I'm AnnaMaria, Melanie's fiancée," she said, extending her hand.

"Sorry, no handshakes in our house," he said, taking her into his giant arms and giving her a huge bear hug.

"Uf!" she said as he squeezed the wind out of her.

"So, Melanie, how have you been?" asked Pops.

"Pops, I won't try and kid you. I know what I did in the past, but I've changed...completely changed. I don't drink, I don't smoke, and I'm completely loyal. I wish I could have been that way in the past, but it's behind me. You'll see. I want to prove it to you, if you'll give me a chance."

"No worries. Everybody deserves a second chance."

"I'm glad you feel that way. That's exactly what your daughter and Bella have said."

"Excuse me, all, but I've got to go pee! I can't believe I've got more months to go. I already feel like a bloated cow!" I said, heading for the bathroom.

"You look like it too, my dear wife," Kathleen said, cackling.

"Oh, why don't you get a job and go to work or something?" I retorted.

"Soon, sweetie, soon," she said, comforting me by rubbing my shoulders.

It was a wonderful day together, and the girls got to show off their rings to Martha and Pops. We were sitting at the table after everything was cleaned up, sipping iced tea.

"You know what's the most wonderful thing about Bella's pregnancy?" Kathleen asked the group.

"What?" everybody intoned together.

"She's hornier than a rabbit, twenty-four hours a day."

Martha and the girls grinned, looking down at the table, while Pops spewed iced tea out of his nose.

"Too much information, maybe," ventured AnnaMaria.

"Although, if you promise not to make any noise, she will make love to you," Melanie laughed uproariously.

"What?" Pops asked.

"Sorry, inside joke."

He just shook his head. Pops isn't a prude, but he can be embarrassed.

"Oh, everybody come here quickly! Give me your hands," I yelled.

They all gathered around me, and I had them hold my tummy and feel little Kevin kicking. It felt really strange to have this little being moving inside me; part of me, yet completely independent of me. Finally, we broke up the soiree and went home. Melanie and AnnaMaria hung around our place for about half an hour before driving home with several containers of food. We had several containers for our refrigerator as well. Martha cooked enough food for an entire company of infantrymen! It was an exhausting but very happy family day. The girls were now an official part of our extended family.

❦ ❦ ❦

Christmas at Pfister-Blankenship was, as always, accompanied by a huge party. This year though, instead of buying a dress from a local store, I had to order one from a maternity shop. I wasn't going to miss the party, even if I was seven months pregnant. When I got the call from the store that the dress was in, I went out at lunch to try it on. In the dressing room, I broke down crying. I'm sure the clerk from the store was used to the ridiculous crying fits from ladies in my condition. She quietly knocked on the fitting room door and gently coaxed me out. She told me over and over how fabulous I looked and how well the dress fitted. I took some small comfort in the fact I wouldn't be wearing a cast like I had the first company Christmas party. And at least, I'd still be accompanied by the most beautiful woman in the world, in my opinion.

Kathleen was fully mobile by now. She was running in the streets up to five miles a day and had her wind back. She was doing really well with her free weights too. I'm not sure why she hadn't gone back to the gym yet. I suspect she still had some ghosts to exorcise. She was growing restless. She hadn't worked in months, and she wouldn't talk about it to me. That was the worst part…the communication…or lack of, really. It was crushing me. I knew it was killing her, and that was breaking my heart.

"When do you think you'll see the doctor again?" I casually slipped into our conversation.

"I go and see him day after tomorrow."

"Do you think he'll clear you to go to work?"

"He might. I've been recording my workouts in a diary since I began the treadmill. I guess I should have told you about that. I meant to. I mean, I wasn't trying to hide it from you. I guess I just didn't, that's all."

"That was a good idea. That way you can show it to him and prove that you're ready to go back to work."

"The hard part is the flight surgeon. You know I still get vertigo occasionally, right?" she put to me.

"No, you've never mentioned it. Why is it you've never shared all this with me? You've never withheld anything from me in the past. What gives?"

"I don't know. It's like I don't want to jinx anything."

"Baby, you know I always have your back. Your secrets are safe with me," I said as I reached across the table and cupped her hand in mine.

She squeezed my hand in response.

"I think I need some cheering up tonight," she said to me with a sidelong glance, tilting her head to one side.

"Does my baby need me to make love to her tonight?"

"No, I think I need to you to fuck me long and hard until the sun comes up!"

I pushed back my half-finished plate and stood up, nearly knocking the chair over. I grabbed my beautiful wife's hands, pulled her up, and dragged her up the stairs in a most wanton fashion. She was right. Since I got pregnant I was horny as a rabbit, and those were the only words I needed to hear. I granted her wish. Not quite until dawn, but very nearly so. At about four in the morning, we finally drifted off to sleep, each of us coated in a light sheen of sweat, breathing heavily, covered in our sheet, heartbeats pounding against each other, as much in love as the first day we met. Life was as perfect in that moment as it could ever be. Me, Kathleen, and little Kevin, kicking away almost as if to say, 'Don't forget me, I'm right here!'

❦ ❦ ❦

Kathleen's doctor cleared her for work. Since she was still occasionally having bouts with vertigo and she couldn't lie to the flight surgeon, she didn't bother making an appointment. It was bad enough that once, while she was driving, she had to pull off the road and into a parking lot until it passed. I could tell she was getting more miserable and restless by the day.

The Christmas ball was a diversion for her. We had a genuinely good time. I got many compliments on my dress, even though I still felt out of place and fat as a cow. It did manage to cheer me up a bit, and Kathleen couldn't keep her hands off me all night. She was forever holding my arm, rubbing my tummy, caressing my cheek, and tucking a strand of hair behind my ear. She pretended not to let it bother her that everybody was showering her with pity, asking her about her accident, asking how she was healing, asking whether she was working again and everything else that went with that line of interrogation.

About four days later, I came home from work to find Kathleen running on the treadmill downstairs. I went down to give her a kiss, but she didn't acknowledge me. She had that look on her face of total concentration. Her eyes were like lasers, staring intently off into space. I went back upstairs and glanced into the kitchen. The chairs were scattered about, and the table was turned on its top, broken in half. I started cringing inwardly, wondering what had set Kathleen off. I had never witnessed a violent act from her in our entire time together.

I went back downstairs to confront her, but she just kept running.

"Kathleen!"

She said nothing, continuing her workout. I reached around behind her and unplugged the machine, listening as the motor cut off instantaneously, nearly causing her to fall.

"How long have you been down here running?" I asked her pointedly.

"About an hour and a half," she said, looking at her watch.

"What happened?"

"Nothing 'happened.' I just needed to run."

"Then, did a magician go through our kitchen and wave a wand, causing all the destruction and mayhem?"

She was leaning forward, bent at the waist, breathing like she'd just run a marathon. Which in point, since she'd been running at that pace for an hour and a half, she'd run more than a half marathon.

"I got a letter today."

"From whom?"

"From the highway patrol."

"And?"

"My temporary replacement has been converted to permanent. I no longer have a job to go back to."

"Oh, baby, I'm so sorry," I said, moving in behind her, rubbing her back, trying to soothe her.

"Fuck it."

"Look, there are plenty of other jobs. There is still LifeFlight...There are ambulance crews...Maybe even back with St. Paul, huh?"

"That's not what I want!"

"Why don't you go take a shower and I'll fix dinner?"

"We can't eat dinner."

"Why not?"

"The table fell down and went boom."

I started laughing at her, hugging her, and I was getting all sweaty. I hauled her upstairs and tried to get her to let me take a shower with her, but she would have no part of it. I didn't want to press her now, so I just left her alone. I went in the kitchen and took the table pieces to the front porch. I lined the chairs up in the space where the table usually sat. I wasn't really in the mood to cook dinner. I knew for sure Kathleen wasn't going to cook, and after her ten to fifteen miles of running she'd need to load up on some energy, so I got out some hamburger to defrost in the microwave and began making spaghetti sauce, just the way she taught me.

As we were eating dinner on the couch, Kathleen turned to me.

"You do realize that since I'm cleared to return to work I'm no longer on temporary disability, and my income will go away?"

"Don't worry. I make plenty of money. And you'll find work, I know you will."

"If I get an ambulance job, though, it won't be shift work. I will be a new member, and it will be a night job. It will totally suck."

"Yeah, but we'll still be able to have dinner together every night. And look at it this way, if you sleep during the day and we make love in the evening, it will be like morning sex for you, right?"

I tried to laugh a little, but Kathleen wasn't having it. She was in a really bad place right now. I set my plate on the coffee table, then took hers out of her hands and placed it next to mine. I tried to straddle her lap, but it didn't work too well since little Kevin was in the way.

"It seems to me, we used to fit together a lot better than this not too very long ago, didn't we?" I joked with Kathleen.

"Well, if you didn't eat the entire refrigerator every damn day and get so fat, it wouldn't be a problem!"

I knew Kathleen was joking, but my hormones were messing with my mind. It started with tears rolling down my cheeks, then with little sobs, then with my shoulders shaking, then came outright crying. Instead of taking pity on me like Kathleen usually did, she surprised me.

"Oh, for God's sake. You know I was just kidding. Would you just shut up!" she yelled at me.

I sat there for a minute, blinking at her, tears still streaming. She pushed at me to get me off her, which I did in a New York minute.

"I told you before that you'd never, ever talk to me that way again. Do you hear me? You get out of this house right now. Do you hear me? Get out! Take your keys and your coat and get out!" I screamed at her at the top of my lungs, pointing to the front door, stamping my foot.

Kathleen had a look of total surprise on her face. I know she was going through a really rough time right now, but I'd be damned if she was going to start with this shit again. I told her before exactly what was going to happen if she did it again. She scrambled for her keys, put on her coat, and was out the door. I heard her SUV start up and drive off. I was still sobbing like a little baby when I picked up the phone. I called Pops.

"Hey, Bells. How are you?" he answered.

Through my tears and crying, I told him that I wanted to talk to Martha. He didn't question me, just gave the phone to her.

"Hello, is that you, Bella?"

"Martha, Kathleen has started up again with her belligerent attitude. If she ends up coming over there, make her sleep on your couch. Under no circumstances are you to let her come back home tonight. Do you hear me?" I practically yelled.

"Bella, are you all right? I'm more worried about you right now. You are eight months pregnant. Do you want me to come over there and sleep in the guest room with you? I'd be more than happy to."

"If you wouldn't mind. I'd rather not be alone right now. That would be wonderful. I'm so sorry to drag you into this."

"Pish-posh. Don't be silly. I'll be over there in about half an hour."

When she got to our house, I poured juice, and we sat on the couch and talked until almost midnight. I had determined I was working from home in the morning starting about ten o'clock, so I'd already called Courtney and let her know.

❦ ❦ ❦

Kathleen stood on Pops' porch and hesitated before ringing the doorbell, but he'd heard her drive up. He opened the door and invited her in.

"Kathleen, I think you messed up. Big time."

"Yeah, I know."

"Well, what are you going to do about it?"

"I've been driving around now for about two and a half hours, trying to think. About Bella…About work…About little Kevin…About life…I'm just…."

"Confused?"

"Yeah. I guess."

"You've been in complete control from the age of twelve. You're now thirty. How is it that you aren't in control now? I mean, what's stopping you from taking all the gifts you have and accepting the fact that you're truly blessed with one of the most perfect women on the face of the planet, so you can just get over yourself?"

"Oh, not you too, Pops!"

"Look, I've never held back in the past, and I'm not about to start now. You need to make this thing right, and you need to make it right, now."

"I was thinking about some flowers," she sighed.

"I don't think that alone is going to do it."

"I also stopped by Allina on the way over here. They've got some openings. I'm going by there tomorrow during the day and fill out the paperwork. I should be working within a couple of days. It'll be straight night shifts, but at least I'll be back at work. That will calm me back down, and that will make Bella feel better, knowing that what was bothering me when I blew up will be under control."

"Well, Kitten, let me suggest something. Wait until tomorrow, after you've gone to Allina, after you've gotten the job, after you've gotten the flowers, and then talk to Bella. Stay here tonight. Let the ladies gossip and comfort each other. Give them some space and let the pressure cooker blow off some steam. What do you say?"

"I'd say, I love you, Pops," she said, giving him a huge hug.

"I love you too, Kitten. Don't worry, everything will be all right. Bella is a good, level-headed woman, but you'll have to prove to her that you're worthy of being let out of the dog house."

"You're right, Pops, as usual."

❀ ❀ ❀

"Courtney Braun."

"Hey, Courtney, it's Kathleen. Look, I think I screwed up big time. Again. Is Bella there? Don't transfer me, I just need to know if she's in the office today."

"I shouldn't even be talking to you, you know. I should be putting bamboo shoots under your fingernails. What in the world did you do to her?"

"Long story. Anyway, is she in today, or is she working from home?"

"She's working from home."

"Okay. Thanks. Don't tell her I called, okay?"

"If you say so. You better offer her an olive branch jiffy-quick!"

"That's what I'm in the process of doing. Thanks. Bye."

"Bye-bye."

Kathleen hung up her phone and started driving home, her new uniforms laying neatly across the back seat of her vehicle, the six dozen daisies nestled in the passenger's seat. She pulled up in the driveway beside my SUV and got out, slinging the uniforms over her shoulder with one hand and gathering up the flowers in her other hand. She mounted the porch steps and instead of using her keys to open the door, she stood in front of the door and rang the doorbell.

When I opened the door and saw it was Kathleen, a mixed bag of emotions crossed my face: I was glad to see her because I loved her so much; Anger for her treating me so badly; Uncertainty....

"Do you think a handful of flowers is going to make everything all right, as beautiful as that display is?" Knowing that daisies were my favorite flowers.

"These are for you, and these are for me," she said, handing the flowers to me on the first part of her sentence and holding up her uniforms on the latter part, smiling feebly at me.

"So, you got a job?"

"Paramedic for Allina here in St. Paul. I hope you won't mind me working nights. Of course, it will mean that we will have morning sex all the time...hopefully all the time...if you'll have me."

I slowly walked up to her, my flowers cradled in my arm, and put my other arm around her, holding her to me. I softly kissed her in the crook of her neck, over and over.

"My whole life, I've gotten what I've gone after. It's always worked, and the timing has always been just right. Now, it's stopped working, and I feel like my life is out of control. It's not like I don't appreciate what I have, I do. I have you. I have little Kevin. I'm overjoyed, but I just feel like I'm spinning in this uncontrolled spiral. I figured it's going to be starting over. I'm waiting for the timing again, and that's just the way it has to be for now. In the meanwhile, I'll play with the baby in the evenings, enjoy dinner with you, and go to work when the bats and the monsters come out at night. Who knows, maybe I'll come across a beautiful young woman from a southern state who is new to the area, doesn't know how to navigate on the snow and ice, and falls and hurts herself," Kathleen said with a broad smile.

I reared back with my free arm and punched her as hard as I could in the arm. Of course, to her it was nothing but a gnat bite, she was so strong.

"That was mean!" I cried.

"You know there will never be anyone else for me as long as I live. Never."

"Never? What if something happened to me, though? I'd want you to remarry. That would be a different case."

"I'd never remarry. You're my wife forever. Remember the death do us part vow? I meant until the death of both of us, sweetie…both of us. You are so perfect. Nobody could ever take your place. For starters, I'd have to take time off and go to Houston to find a gay woman with your accent," she said with a laugh.

"When are you ever going to get over the fact that you are the one with the accent and not me?" I said, now fully relaxed.

I felt at this moment, thinking back, that I had my Kathleen for the first time since the accident. She'd been in a better mood sometimes, but for the first time she was truly back, even if it wasn't the job she wanted.

"So, when do you start?"

"Uh, yeah, that's the thing. We're really short-handed. I go in tonight at eleven. I work eleven to seven."

"UH! That's not fair! Tonight?" I said, stamping my foot.

"I have to earn a paycheck. By the way, I'll actually be getting a decent check, more than I thought I would. It's more than St. Paul. Less than the highway patrol, of course, but it's adequate money. I'll still be a kept woman with your six-figure income, but I don't mind, so long as I'm being kept by you," she said with a smile.

"Let me put these in water, and we can go lie down for a while. I'm pretty tired. I've had a rough day. And you can get a nap to transition you into nights."

"Sounds good to me."

While we were lying in bed, Kathleen squirted several gobs of hand lotion into her hand and let it warm up. Then she pulled up my shirt and began to rub it into my humungous, fat belly. She kept rubbing and rubbing, and it felt so good I finally fell asleep, although little Kevin was at it the whole time, letting his presence be known, kicking and scuffling, punching and fighting. That was getting old. I was ready to have him yanked out of my body. I already loved him so much, but I was done!

My eyes fluttered open sometime later, and Kathleen was lying directly by my side, propped up on one arm, looking directly at my face.

"What?"

"Nothing. I'm just looking at you."

"Stop!"

"Why? I like looking at you."

"You're freaking me out!"

"The good news is, and I don't know how I lucked out, I don't work on the weekends. I start on Sunday night and work through Thursday night. So, this weekend we're going to take one last romp up on the North Shore as childless adults while we still can. There's only about a foot of snow, so it's still easy to get around. You up for it?'

"If you'll quit staring at me. At least blink."

"Does this help?" Kathleen asked as she slipped her hand under the waistband of my shorts.

"Stop."

"Or maybe this?" as she began moving around in earnest.

"I'm not in the mood."

"Or maybe this..." she said as she entered me.

"Oh, Kathleen..." I said as I reached up for her lips with mine, caressing them with my tongue, getting hotter by the second.

"I thought so," she mumbled into my mouth.

※ ※ ※

"Here's your lunch, baby," I said, holding up her insulated tote.

"What did you pack me?"

"Two cotto salami sandwiches, two apples, a banana, two power bars, two juices, two bottles of water, and some gum. You're going to spend your entire paycheck just on your lunch if you don't watch it!"

"You're funny. Are you going to miss me?"

"Baby, I miss you even when you're just downstairs working out."

"Oh, you do not."

"I'm serious. I do."

She reached up and cupped my cheeks with her hands and lightly danced across my lips with hers, like the Sugar Plum Fairies from the Nutcracker. I melted into her arms.

"Oh, don't get me started. You better go."

"I know. But you know what? After all these months, I'm so glad to be going to work. It's practically sending shivers up and down my spine. Maybe I'll bring you back a severed finger or something as a memento of my first night back."

"You do, and you'll be on the porch in a sleeping bag!" I laughed.

"Bye. Don't stay up too late. Get some sleep."

"I'll try. Just don't send a trooper to wake me up like you did before. I'll never be able to shake those nightmares."

"Do you still have them?"

"Of course. I thought I was going to lose you and my life was over."

"Oh, sweetie, come here."

She enveloped me in her arms one final time before tramping off into the night to become my soldier of the night once again. My Kathleen. Once again in uniform. She was so buff, so tough, and so damn hot! It stirred something deep inside me every time I thought about it.

"Hey, baby. Why are you calling so late?" I answered a few hours later.

"Because it's after two in the morning. I called to tell you to turn out the lights. I knew you'd still be awake."

I had to laugh. My wife knew me pretty well.

"I know. I'm just having a hard time sleeping without you being here."

"Well, you're going to have to get used to it. *Go to sleep!*"

"Okay. For you, I will. Satisfied?"

"If you really mean it."

"Have you been busy?"

"We've only had one call. A bar fight. Total stupidity. We got the bleeding staunched on both of them, got the glass debrided, and got them over to the hospital. Jerks. I'm glad I'm not a man. I mean, there are women that do the same sort of thing, I guess, but statistically, the testosterone poisoning is mostly limited to men. They're both going to be hurting tomorrow when the alcohol wears off."

"You're funny."

"I'm glad you were awake and I got to talk to you. I miss the time that we got to talk when I worked for the fire department. I especially like having two days off that I got to spend with you, but the chatting that I got to do late at night was so special. Even though we were apart, it was like a special little window that you and I had into the world to each other that nobody else could see. I miss that."

"Oh, baby, I'm so glad that you're back. I mean really back. You're whole again. I know this isn't the job that you want, and I know that you'll have to wait a long time for openings, and I know that you may never get to fly again, but I'm so glad that you're back. Thank you again for the flowers. I don't think I've ever heard of anybody getting that many daisies for somebody...ever. I think they are cute as can be!"

"It was a lame gesture trying to make up to you for what I did. You know I didn't mean it. You know I was just trying to wrestle with my inner demons."

"I know. I forgive you. But I'm warning you, this is absolutely the last time. If it happens again, I'm going to the basement, getting your hockey stick, and beating the crap out of you!"

"If I do it again, I'll go down in the basement and get the hockey stick myself and give it to you, and you can beat the crap out of me with my permission!"

We both laughed. We chatted for another fifteen minutes before she said she had to go because they were pulling out of the hospital. I was sad that she had to go, but it was what she did. Now, satisfied, I reached over and turned off the light. I think I was asleep in moments, with a smile on my face.

※ ※ ※

I had to leave in the morning by seven o'clock, not getting to see Kathleen, not getting to welcome her into my arms, not getting to see her home after her first night back to work. So, I wrote her a two-page, handwritten letter and left it on the kitchen counter where she would see it when she cooked her breakfast. I was pretty sure she'd scramble some eggs when she got home; she normally did. I was sort of melancholy for not seeing her, but my attention was taken over by little Kevin. He'd given me the worst case of heartburn I'd ever had in my entire life. I was chewing antacids every two hours through the night. His tiny feet were playing a drum line on the inside of my stomach all night long without stopping for five minutes at a time. I'd had enough. I was going to practically beg the doctor today to do an early C-section. It would only be three weeks early, after all. That shouldn't be a problem. I knew I wouldn't end up calling because the answer would be no, but I sure as hell wanted to.

When she got up early on Saturday to drive us up to the north shore, I was on the verge of telling Kathleen not just 'No' but 'Hell no!' I didn't relish sitting in the car and having to pee every twenty-five minutes. I didn't relish being bounced around. I just plain didn't want to go. But I wasn't about to say anything. Kathleen was back to normal, and that was enough for me. I packed an overnight bag, and in the very top of it I put three small, plastic trash can liners, just in case I needed to hurl. And I added an entirely new bottle of antacids for that little brat Kevin and what he'd been doing to me.

"Kathleen, I have only one requirement."

"What's that, sweetie?" she asked.

"The hotel at Two Harbors. No tents. No floors. No ground. Just not happening this weekend."

"Okay, I have no problem with that, you wimp."

"Yeah, a nearly eight and a half months pregnant wimp to you, lady!" I laughed and punched her.

We took off on Friday around ten o'clock and made it to Duluth just after lunch. We ate a sub sandwich at a deli, then took the shoreline drive to look at the lake. We got off at Tetagouche and 'hiked' into the falls; it's a walk on an asphalt paved footpath. Despite the foot of snow on the ground it was pretty easy going. There wasn't any ice anywhere and they cleared the snow every few hours for the visitors. After we finished there, we drove a little farther up the shore to the cliffs overlooking Superior.

About two or three miles south of Knife River, we stopped the car to get out for a stretch of the legs. I don't know why, but I felt something ominous was in the air.

We walked to the iron-filled cliffs overlooking the lake and took in a marvelous view. To me, this was just as wonderful as my trip to the Grand Canyon. There was a light breeze, the temperature was perfect, and the sun was glimmering off the ice on the lake in all its broken floes.

Kathleen kept walking closer and closer to the edge. Personally, I'm not so good with heights, but I knew she must have been up that high many times as a firefighter and then being in the rescue flights. Then the knot in my stomach began to tighten. Kathleen kept moving about a half step at a time, slowly, steadily, ever closer to the rim. Suddenly it hit me like a ton of bricks.

I ran up close to her and wrapped my arms around her, squeezing her tightly.

"What the heck are you...?" she sputtered.

"I promised before God and witnesses that I would be with you forever," I answered.

"What are you talking about? Are you crazy? Let go of me. Back off! You know you're afraid of heights!"

"I don't care. You're not backing out on me. You're not going to, you hear me?"

"What do you mean?" she cried out.

"I know what you're doing. If you do it, you'll leave me with the terrible feeling in my heart that I actually watched you. Think about that. You say you love me, but everything you've done since the crash, everything you've said, everything...You're trying to throw me away. How will breaking my heart so hard it will never mend show me that you really love me?"

"You don't understand!" she threw back at me.

"Oh, don't I? Well, how about you explain it, so this little old Texas girl can grasp it a little better? Can you do that, Kathleen? Do you really think that me watching you die is going to make me happy?"

"Who said anything about dying?" she cried.

"Here. Let's make this easy. You take a step, I'll take a step, you, me, you, me…And when we get to the edge, we'll both go together, like Romeo and Juliet."

"Bella, for God's sake! Back off!"

At that point, I remember being pushed backwards, falling on my ass, then hitting my head on something buried in the snow, much the same way as the night I met my beautiful Kathleen: the firefighter…the paramedic…the fighter of wrongs and evils…the giver of all to everyone before helping herself…the magical wonder. Then, everything went crimson, then black…totally black.

When I came to, I was sitting up, being held in place by the seat belt on my side of our SUV, while Kathleen was driving like a maniac toward Duluth. Kathleen's right hand was holding a towel full of ice on the back of my head, which was pounding like nobody's business. She pulled the towel off and I saw what looked like a gallon of blood dripping from it. I was okay until I saw that, then I heaved over my pants, the seat, and onto the floor of the vehicle.

"Okay, it's definite at this point. You've officially managed to get yourself a bad concussion, baby. Hold tight, and we'll get you to the ER as soon as we can. Can you focus on anything with your eyes, or is it blurry?"

I couldn't answer her. For one thing, I couldn't interpret what she was saying. It was like the Charlie Brown specials when an adult talked, and it came out as a muted trumpet: wah, wah-wah-wah, wah-wah, wah-wah.

"What in the fuck did you think you were doing? For that matter, what in the fuck did you think I was doing? *Huh?* Can you answer me?" she was fairly screaming at me, holding the icepack to my head, still lead-footing it down the road.

I couldn't answer. I was barely conscious. It seemed like it took forever to get back to Duluth. She drove up to the emergency room entrance and hopped out, running inside. A nurse came running out with her.

"Victim is eight and a half months pregnant, sustained a concussion in a fall on the rocks up at Knife River, bleeding heavily, has vomited repeatedly, unable to speak, pupils dilated and moderately unresponsive, pulse 110 and thready, don't know on the BP."

"Ms. Pope, do you know if she urinated on herself on the way in?"

"I'm not sure. It's possible. Why?"

"We may have way bigger problems," the nurse said wiping Bella's crotch with her hand and bringing her hand to her nose to sniff it.

"Oh, shit!"

"Oh, shit is right. I think she broke her water. Let's get her inside jiffy quick, get her undressed, and do an exam!"

Kathleen and the nurse got me on the gurney and wheeled me into the emergency room.

"That's okay, ma'am. We can take her from here."

"I'm a paramedic, and this is my wife. I'd rather stay with her, if you don't mind."

"Well, I don't see as that would be a problem then, so long as the doctor doesn't object. I'll get a fresh four-square for her head and you keep that applied. Let me get her pants off and give her an exam."

The nurse pulled off my boots and socks, then my pants and underwear, putting my feet in the stirrups.

"It's official. She's lost her mucous plug. She's only dilated to six centimeters, though, so we've got time. Let's get her head stitched up before we do anything else."

They got my head gash covered in gauze soaked with iodine soap for about fifteen minutes, then the doctor walked in. He worked quickly and gave me fourteen stitches, then turned his attention to the bigger problem.

"So, little lady, you say you want to have a baby today, huh?" he laughed jovially.

I was pretty much out of it still with the concussion.

"Baby?"

"Yup, baby. He's here, knocking on the door, and wanting to get out. So, we're going to go ahead and give you an IV and get an anesthesiologist here just in case. I will tell you this, though, because of your concussion we can't intentionally give you any drugs unless we start experiencing complications. Do you understand me, Bella?"

"What?"

"Bella, can you understand me?"

"Baby? Now? It's not time yet," I managed to stammer.

"Well, now, I don't think he checked your dance card. He's ready and raring to go. You're already six...no, you're at eight centimeters dilated. Do you think you're going to be able to push when the time comes?"

"Push? Yes, push. Already? But he's not supposed to be here...."

"Maybe with that little bump to your head he decided now was the time to come on out and see what his two mommies were doing for the weekend."

I noticed Dr. Finklestein laughed a lot. It was the only thing I could really concentrate on. My head was throbbing and was pulling tightly. I still wasn't sure why Kevin was being born right now, but I had to try and concentrate. At least Kathleen was with me, holding my hand. I wondered where I was. I wondered how I got there. But at least Kathleen was there, so everything must be all right.

"Okay, Bella, time for the first work. When I tell you, I want you to try and bear down, push as much as you can. I know it's going to be hard, and I know it's going to hurt, and it will probably double the intensity of your headache, but I need for you to be a big girl and do the best that you can, right?"

I nodded my head, remembering the classes we'd been to. I looked up into Kathleen's smiling face, then it hit me.

"Dammit, you pushed me down! You're the reason I'm here! You pushed me down and made me hit my head! What are you doing here with me? Get out! Get out! Do you hear me? Get out!"

"Look, Bella, don't you remember? You were trying to push us both over the cliff. I pushed you back to save you and the baby. You fell back, and there was a rock under the snow. I would never have hurt you on purpose. You know that!"

"I did what?"

"You got some strange idea that I was going to jump off the cliff. I was just checking my vertigo with high places, that's all. You went totally Romeo and Juliet on me, and you swore that if I jumped we'd all go together. I have no idea where that came from. I just knew that I didn't want you anywhere near the edge, so I pushed you back. I'm really sorry. I had no way of knowing there was a huge rock under the snow."

"I did that?" I asked demurely.

Kathleen just nodded, rubbing my hand in hers.

"I must have had the worst case of hormone rage in the history of mankind."

"Naw, I've heard of much worse. Trust me. Now, if you don't mind, we missed that contraction completely, and for now, 'Kevin,' as you say, needs all your attention. Care to play along?" laughed the doctor with a big, old belly laugh with his big, old belly.

"Sorry, doctor."

"Any idea of the size through your last ultrasound?" he asked.

"Somewhere in the neighborhood of about eight and a half pounds," said Kathleen.

"Let me give you a little help, then."

He injected my perineum with a local and made a double-angled episiotomy to give the baby's head more room to crown. Even without IV drugs, he could do that much, and I would be ever so grateful later.

I started contracting and pushing, screaming for an epidural, getting told I couldn't have one due to the concussion, begging for a C-section, getting told it was too late, and finally, thirty-five minutes later, I was holding one very messy little boy, refusing to wait until they cleaned him up. He was healthy and crying and he took to my breast like a duck to water.

Crying, I looked to Kathleen who was smiling, looking down at us, with one hand on me and one hand on Kevin's back while he was suckling.

"Well, what do you think, baby?"

"I'm jealous," she said.

"Why would you be jealous of such a precious little thing? Of our baby?"

"Because he's sucking on what were my boobs last week. Now, I guess I have to give them up for a while!"

Everybody in the room thought that was raucously funny and laughed wholeheartedly. I blushed, but I did so with love. I wriggled my finger at Kathleen, indicating that I wanted her to lean in closely, then I whispered into her ear.

"Baby, I'll share, if you don't think it's too gross!"

She just smiled at me and caressed my shoulder. Was it right to be so horny while holding your newborn baby? I almost felt ashamed, but not quite. Kathleen had done that to me since the night I was on the gurney at the hospital when she first rescued me.

"I have a few calls to make. I'll be back in about half an hour. Okay, sweetie?" Kathleen said, bending over the bed.

I leaned up to kiss her, but realized it wasn't me she was kissing, it was Kevin. It brought tears of joys to my eyes. Finally, she kissed me too. We were complete. We were whole. We were a family.

"Hey, Martha. We're in the hospital up in Duluth."

"Oh, my goodness. Is something wrong? Is everybody all right?"

"I clobbered Bella pretty good and gave her a concussion." Kathleen laughed.

"You *what*?"

"I actually did. It was an accident. I'll tell you about it later. I have you and Pops booked in at the Country Inn here in Duluth for three nights. You better get packed if you want to get here in time for dinner tonight."

"What on earth are you talking about?"

"Nine pounds, three ounces."

"Nine pounds, three ounces? Nine pounds, three ounces? Bella has had little Kevin?" she started shouting into the phone.

"That she has. Now, get those bags packed and hit the road!"

"Oh, we sure will. Are you at the hospital now?"

"Of course! Where else would I be?"

"Pops should be home within half an hour, and I'll have us packed. Oh, this is so exciting! I'm a grandma!"

"Hey, Martha? You're also a mom. A darned good one. With two daughters," Kathleen added.

Kathleen could hear her start to cry over the phone.

"Bye now. I have to make a few more calls," Kathleen told her, then quickly dialed Courtney.

"This is Courtney."

"Hey, Courtney. Kathleen."

"Oh, hi. What's up?"

"They wouldn't let Bella have any meds because I gave her a concussion."

"What?"

"Yeah, up on the cliffs today, I knocked her down and there was a rock under the snow. She hit her head. Bled like a pig. Got fourteen stitches. She did get a double episiotomy though, so that helped."

"Episiotomy. Then…."

"Yooper. Nine pounds, three ounces."

"Oh, my God! She's had him?"

"Sort of seems that way, doesn't it? We're up here in Duluth. Sort of turned into an emergency with the concussion and breaking her water and all. Next thing you know, they'll probably want to haul me in on domestic assault charges. You might want to go ahead and process her maternity paperwork for her. We'll be back in St. Paul in about three days, I expect, and she can fax whatever you need then…signatures, whatever. I'm sure she'll call you later tonight when she's back in her right mind. It was sort of funny. She was totally out of it at first. When she started coming around, she realized I was the one that pushed her down. Then she started screaming at me to get out. I had to remind her that she was the one that got this funny idea into her head that I was inching up on the precipice to jump off, and she went totally nuts on me and grabbed me around the waist and said if I was going to jump, we were going together," Kathleen laughed.

"Little Miss 'I'm Afraid of Heights' did that?" Courtney said with a gasp.

"Hormones, I'm guessing. I've been having a problem with vertigo, and I wanted to see if heights bothered me or if it was unrelated. It's confirmed. It's not related to heights. Anyway, Kevin's doing great. Healthy as can be. You can come by the house later this week if you want to see him...or not."

"Oh, you can bet your little red wagon I'll be by to see him as soon as you get home. Do you need me to do anything at the house for him? You all ready?"

"We've got everything there. I just have to assemble his bed. The playpen is downstairs, and it just folds out. We don't have a changing table. It seemed silly. We'll just use his bed."

"Well, thanks for calling. I know you're busy there. Give Bella my love. And you too."

"Thanks. Bye now."

"Hello?" Melanie answered the phone next.

"Are they keeping you busy already?" Kathleen answered back.

"Oh, my gracious, Kathleen. It's only the first weekend, and we've done nothing but study! Well, we did find time to sneak under the covers and cuddle up on Friday night, but man! This isn't going to be any walk in the park! But when we're done, we're going to be so ready to conquer the world. So, what's going on with you and Bella?"

"We were up messing around in Duluth and her water broke. You and AnnaMaria are aunties."

Kathleen guessed that both had been listening because they both started screaming like a couple of little schoolgirls.

"We'll be back in St. Paul in about three days. We'll have you over for dinner, and you can play with Kevin. Sound like a plan?"

"Wouldn't miss it for the world. And Kathleen?" she said, her voice suddenly getting very quiet and starting to quiver.

"What, Cricket?"

"You haven't called me Cricket in forever...."

"I...I honestly don't know where that came from. Does it bother you?"

"No, I like it. It's just that...It's just...I'm so, so sorry, Kathleen..." and she began to break down and cry.

"Melanie, you've got to forgive yourself. It isn't healthy for you, and it's not healthy for AnnaMaria. She's going to be your wife...forever. And I've already forgiven you...forever. So, let's have no more of this. Okie-dokey?"

"Okay, just give us a call, and we'll be there. We're both so happy for you."

The last call Kathleen made was to Allina, letting them know that I'd just had my baby, and she wouldn't be in until Wednesday night. They had no problem whatsoever and told her to take as much time as needed, but to come straight into the pediatrics office as soon as we got back to the cities.

Kathleen showed up at the room they'd put me in upstairs. There was a puzzled look on her face since the door was closed and there was a woman in the room talking with me. It was a social worker. Kathleen understood it quickly, and her shoulders fell. She walked away from the room, presumably heading for a waiting room. The social worker was trying to get me to say that Kathleen had assaulted me, and she wanted me to say that I felt in danger, which was the furthest thing from the truth. I kept explaining over and over what had happened, but she didn't believe me. I'm sure there are many abused wives and children that make up stories, but this was the truth. I finally told her to go get a Duluth police officer with a polygraph machine or leave me alone. Grudgingly, she left, making me sign a report. I carefully read the report first, making sure it read exactly the way I'd told her.

Kathleen walked into the room with her hands buried in her pockets.

"So, am I going to jail?"

"Not this time. But try that shit again and you just might." I snickered.

"What made you think I was going to jump off that damn thing anyway?"

"You'd just been really depressed lately and had a faraway look in your eye. Oh, I don't know. Call it watching one too many movies or something. Plus, you have wigged out on me a couple of times. No explanation, no reason. Just plain gone off the deep end."

"Yeah, well, I've gotten control of that now. For real. Not what I want, not where I want to be, but in control. And I do like working the cases we get on the ambulance. I know it's only been a week, but there's just something about helping somebody who's been in a wreck or somebody that's had a heart attack or any of the situations we deal with. There are going to be people that you lose, but that's part of life. You have to think about the vast majority where you improve the quality of their life by being there in eight minutes, which is our target...."

Kathleen tapered off when I opened my gown and started squeezing my breast. It squirted a small trail of milk in the air. She was absolutely enamored by the sight of it.

"Amazing, isn't it?" I asked.

"You've got to stop. That's wasteful," she said.

"Nuh-uh. I told you I'd share. Come here, baby."

Kathleen's eyes were glazed over. Moving ever so slowly, she got up and shut the door to the room. Too bad it didn't have a lock. She leaned over the bed and slowly put her lips over my nipple, taking it fully in her mouth, and beginning to suckle. I gently put my hand on the back of her head. She kept it up for several minutes, then sat back in the chair by the bed.

"How is it?" I asked.

"It's...It's...."

"Well?"

"Magical."

I laughed at her, cupping her cheek in my hand.

"You want to know the worst part? I must be the worst mother in the world."

"Why do you say that?" asked Kathleen.

"Because I'm so damned horny right now I can't stand it. When Kevin breast fed it was so normal, so right. But when you did it, it sent me through the roof. I'm so wet."

"Let me take care of that for you, then," Kathleen offered.

"Remember, you can't go inside me."

"I don't intend to."

She slipped her hand under the covers and within minutes started to bring me to bliss, and continued over and over, but soon enough, a nurse walked through the door to take my vital signs. Kathleen whipped her hand back quickly and stood by the side of the bed.

"Sorry, I'll get out of your way, so you can work," Kathleen ventured.

"Don't worry, I won't be a minute," said the nurse.

The nurse had a growing smile on her face. It was evident she could smell my essence in the room. I was never so embarrassed in my life. She did what she needed to do and was just about to exit the room when she turned back.

"Ladies, remember you can't have any penetration for six weeks. Play is okay, just no penetration."

I literally covered my face with my hands. I wanted to die right there on the spot. Then she leaned down and lowered her voice to a whisper.

"I didn't even wait three weeks. I'm a bit of a horn dog myself!" she let out as she left the room whistling.

"I don't care how much I beg, don't ever do that again while we're here in the hospital. I don't think I could take that again!" I said, groaning.

"Do the people at your office know that besides being the penultimate professional you're also a total slut?"

I held out my hands for Kathleen who walked back over to the bed and took mine in hers.

"That's right. I am a total slut. But just for you, baby. I have been since the first day you walked into my bedroom wearing your tee shirt and panties, flexing those beautiful thighs, and letting me rub them. You had me right there. I mean, you had my heart going pitty-pat in the hospital the night before, but that morning, you had my heart in your hands and my slutty ways just oozing to get to you."

"Slag!"

"That's me, baby."

Kathleen leaned across the bed and kissed me like she hadn't seen me for weeks. It was such a wonderful feeling, like the stars had all begun to fall from the sky at once, and I was standing on the lawn in the middle of summer, watching it all. My stomach was doing flip flops. Speaking of my stomach….

"I expect you, as my personal trainer, to do something about this!" I said as I took a handful of skin from my stomach and rolled it back and forth.

"I will. And I won't go all drill instructor on you either. Slow and steady, that's what will do it. Before long, you'll have your perfect body back. Six months tops."

"Six months?" I whined.

"You want to go slow and steady. Who's the expert here? Just like rebuilding my body. Slow and steady," Kathleen admonished.

"Oh, slow and steady, like running fifteen miles?" I reminded her.

"At least it finally helped me clear my head and get things right, didn't it?"

"Go to the nursery and get Kevin. I don't care if he's sleeping or not. I want him here with us."

"Will do. See you in a sec."

❀ ❀ ❀

We got home Tuesday afternoon. Kathleen took the car carrier in first with little Kevin and was surprised to see the playpen already set up. At first, she thought of Pops, but they'd not left Duluth until this morning, so it wasn't him. Then she came and helped me up the steps since I was still a little wobbly on my feet. When we got upstairs, I went to lie down for a while. Kathleen went into the guest bedroom/nursery.

"Hey, Bella. Come in here."

"I just want to lie down. I'm beat."

"I think you better come in here."

I struggled to get up off the bed and walked into the room where Kathleen stood. The dresser had been moved to the outer wall against the window. And there was the crib, all put together. And next to it was a matching changing table, also put together. Both had sheets and blankets that matched. And the curtains had been changed to match as well. Kathleen pulled out her phone.

"Hey, Kathleen. Whatcha up to?"

"Thank you, Scott. I want you to know we really appreciate the work that you and Eileen did for us. And for getting the changing table. You guys are great," Kathleen said.

"What are you talking about?"

"Didn't you come over and set this up? You're the only one with a key."

"Have you been drinking, girl? Start at the beginning and tell me what you're going on about."

"You really didn't do this?"

"You're talking gibberish."

"Oh. Never mind, then. I'll talk to you later. I was going to tell everybody at the station anyway. You want to spread the word? Bella had the baby. Kevin Steven Pope. Nine pounds, three ounces. Late Saturday afternoon."

"That's great! Congratulations!"

"Thanks. I'll talk to you later, Scott."

"Okay. I'll let everybody know."

"Bye."

I was still running my hands over the changing table, wondering who brought it to us if it wasn't Scotty and his wife.

"I think for dinner I just want a sandwich and some chips. That all right with you?" I asked Kathleen.

"Sounds groovy. I'll go down and make it right now."

"No, I want to make it. I haven't been doing much of anything lately, and I want to do it."

"Sure. Call me when it's ready."

I went downstairs and into the kitchen.

"Hey, Kathleen!" I shouted.

"What do you need, sweetie? Change your mind and want me to make the sandwiches?"

"I think you better come down here!"

I heard her come galloping down the stairs and into the kitchen. Then, she was staring with her mouth open just like I was. Instead of our usual four chairs there were now six: two larger chairs that matched the others, now surrounded a brand-new wooden table with a leaf in the middle.

"Okay, this is getting ridiculous. Who in the hell are the furniture elves? I figured it was Scott and Eileen. First off, it's something they would do. Secondly, they have a key. But they didn't even know you had the baby. This is a little bit spooky. Maybe Courtney? She has a key, doesn't she?" Kathleen ventured.

I pulled out my cell phone.

"Hey, Bella. How do you feel? When are you coming home?"

"We came home this afternoon, Courtney. Have you been over, or have you sent somebody to my house?" I asked.

"What? Why would I?"

"I'm being serious here. I need to know if you had something done here."

"I am being serious. I have no idea what you're talking about."

"Somebody came in, put the crib together, bought us a changing table, set the playpen up, and bought us a new kitchen table and two more chairs."

"They did *what?*"

"You heard me. We have no idea who it was. This is seriously weird. We appreciate it, but we want to know who did it."

"Well it wasn't me or anybody I know."

"Okay, thanks. I'll talk to you tomorrow."

"Bye-bye."

Kathleen and I just stood looking at each other. It was a weird feeling. Grateful for having gotten the gifts, but almost a feeling of being violated for not having the knowledge of who had been in our house. We both almost jumped out of our skin when the doorbell rang. I was surprised that it didn't wake up Kevin who was still asleep in the playpen. Kathleen answered the door and standing in the doorway were Melanie and AnnaMaria.

"It's freezing out here. Can we come in?" giggled AnnaMaria.

Kathleen waved them in the doorway and took their coats. They kicked off their boots and left them on the rug in front of the door.

"Oh, look, he's sleeping! Isn't he so cute!" squealed Melanie.

"He won't be if you keep making noises like that!" I said, shushing her.

Kevin started grunting and rooting like a little piglet. I had to admit, he was very cute. I walked over to the playpen and picked him up to see if we could get him to wake up. It didn't take very long until he opened his eyes and started to make suckling motions. I moved to the easy chair and put him on my breast, covering him with a blanket.

"Have you two eaten dinner yet?" asked AnnaMaria.

"Actually, we were just about to make some sandwiches and eat some chips. Would you like some? We have salami, ham, and roast beef," Kathleen said.

"Maybe after Kevin's finished with dinner we can all go sit at the new table and eat together," giggled Melanie like a junior high school girl.

They had both been laughing nonstop since they'd shown up. I knew they were pretty happy these days, but something was up. Then, it hit me.

"What table?" I asked.

"The one in your kitchen, silly."

"Where did it come from?"

"Ikea. Same with the changing table."

"You girls bought those for us? How did you get in the house?"

"The key under the brick in front. Remember, from when you let me stay here when they were trying to commit me? We just wanted to do something nice for you."

"How did you know about the kitchen table though? How did you know that I broke it?" asked Kathleen.

"You broke it? Wow. We didn't. We just brought in the changing table and saw the table was gone, so we went back to the store."

"But you guys put everything together?"

"Yeah, my grandpa always had me help him working on stuff before he died. I lived with him and my grandmother until they died when I was eight and they put me into the system. I'm pretty handy with a screwdriver and a wrench," said AnnaMaria.

"I don't know how we can thank you two. Seriously. That was so thoughtful of you."

"Compared to what you did for us? It was nothing."

"I think Kevin's about done here. He's stopped sucking. Kathleen, would you get me a towel, please. Do you want to hold him?" I said after getting him to burp.

Melanie shot up off the couch like a bullet with her arms out. She gently took Kevin in her hands and walked back over to AnnaMaria and cradled him between the two of them. They both looked down on him with adoration, tickling him, rolling him back and forth, pinching him lightly, and getting him to smile.

Kathleen went into the kitchen to start making sandwiches after taking everybody's order. AnnaMaria got up and followed her.

"Kathleen, can I ask you something?" she asked.

"Sure. What is it?"

"Well, you and Melanie were together for three years, right?"

"Yes. I was twenty-three and she was eighteen when we started dating."

"And now, you're friends again."

"I'd like to think so."

"Do you ever…think about her?"

"Well, sure."

"I mean, do you ever think about…."

"I think what you're trying to ask is do I ever think about her in a romantic sense, right?"

"Erm, yeah."

"Of course. You can't spend three years with somebody in that sense and never think about it. But do I think about having any romantic connection with her now? Not at all. I have fond memories of the past, but it's in the past. And I try and only remember the good things, not the bad things. When we were together, she smoked, drank, cursed worse than a sailor, so many things. Mostly, she was totally insecure and that was her way of making the world think she was all grown up. What you have is a much better person. What you two have is so much more special. There's no need for you to worry. She's totally in love with you, and only you. And I'm totally in love with Bella, and only her. Okay?"

Kathleen gave her a hug, which made her feel so much better for having the conversation. I could hear what they were saying, and it made me feel all fuzzy inside knowing that my Kathleen was such a good person, almost like an older sister.

We all ate at the table. I cradled Kevin in my lap and ate with one hand. We talked and laughed and had a happy dinner. Finally, the girls said they had to go home and do a slew of homework. We said our goodbyes, and they left for the evening. Kathleen got a look in her eye, one I knew only too well.

"What's going on?" I asked her.

"What do you mean?" she replied.

"Don't give me that. I can see the wheels turning in your head. What's going on?"

She took Kevin from me and kissed his head, rocking him back and forth.

"Want to have sex?" she asked.

"Yes, but that's not the point. I asked you a question."

"Let me put Kevin down, then let's go upstairs."

"Kathleen, stop it. What are you thinking?" I asked, exasperatedly.

"You'll see. Just wait."

※ ※ ※

Kathleen and I had laid down for a nap at eight thirty. Her watch alarm went off at ten o'clock, and we'd been hard asleep the whole time.

"I thought you were going to make love to me," I asked.

"I did. In my dreams. But now, I have to act like a grown up and go to work, and I still have to pack my lunch."

"You go take a shower and let me do that, baby," I said, just as Kevin started squirming and fussing in his crib.

"Or not," Kathleen said, smiling.

She went into the nursery and checked him. She changed his poopy diaper, then brought him in to me with a burp rag. He was only about four weeks old and was already enjoying Kathleen tossing him lightly in the air and catching him. He wasn't quite laughing, but he would coo when she did it, then she would plaster his face full of kisses. When she laid him on my chest, his little mouth was like a magnet. He started sucking immediately for all he was worth. I let out a deep sigh.

"What's the matter, sweetie?"

"I think I'm going to go ahead and take three months off work instead of six weeks. I'm just not going to be ready. I'm enjoying this too much," I said.

"Just do a mixed feeding. Express your milk for bottles during the daytime with the nanny, then at night nurse him. You could do that for several months. Just out of curiosity, do you think you'll get to keep them?"

"Keep what?" I pondered.

"Your ginormous boobs. They must be three sizes bigger than before you got pregnant. You know, if you keep them they'll sag. That's why mostly I hope they go back. Not that I'd mind if you keep them and they sag. I'd love your body no matter what."

"That's a backhanded compliment if I've ever heard one," I said with a bit of an icy glare.

"Look, I get it. Pregnancy does things to a woman's body. Your hips spread, your body changes here and there, your facial features are larger than they were before. And a lot of it is preparing you for future kids, so you'll have more fat reserves to ensure the next child is healthy. But don't you worry, your personal trainer is here. My goal is not to make you what you were before, my goal is to make you as healthy as you can be. So, you need to get into that mindset too. Not rebuild. Build. Got it?"

"Aye, aye, mon capitan!" I saluted her.

Kathleen moved downstairs and packed her lunch, then returned upstairs and got her uniform on.

"Oh, and I have a special surprise for you when I get off work today," Kathleen blurted out.

"What is it?" I asked her.

"Can't tell. It's a surprise. I have a stop to make on the way home, and I probably won't be home until about eleven o'clock or so."

"Why so late?"

"You'll just have to be patient."

I hated it when she told me she had a surprise and then made me wait so long to find out what it was. It made it harder for me to sleep. The next day, I watched the clock all morning as I played with Kevin. Eleven rolled past...then twelve...then one. I was beginning to get a bit worried, then I heard the key in the door. In walked Kathleen, but what I saw astounded me.

"Well, what do you think? I quit Allina," Kathleen said, pirouetting in her new jumpsuit.

"Kathleen...I...I..." I stuttered.

"Medic 8. It's southwest a little, over in district two. Nice, huh?"

"You mean, you're back with St. Paul?"

"Back to my roots. I've had Reed and a couple of others looking out. And I kept all seniority and time in service, so I went to the head of the hiring class. That, and no more vertigo. After all, I'm still a firefighter. And...I got 'B' shift. I get time off with all my friends from Station 7. Would you imagine that?"

"Kathleen Marie! Would it have hurt you to talk to me about what you were doing? This is exactly the type of thing that's been bothering me! Life-altering decisions that you don't include me in anymore!" I huffed at her.

"The position didn't open up until last week. I was fast-tracked. I had no idea that I would get pulled in because there were thirty-five applicants. I just called in yesterday and was told to show up this morning. It just happened in a whirlwind. I didn't want to jinx it, and I wanted to truly surprise you. That's all. I didn't mean to hurt your feelings," she said with a whimper.

"It's not that. It's just that you don't include me in anything anymore, it seems."

"Okay. The other day when you saw the wheels turning in my head? We're going to rent out the civic center. We're going to buy Melanie and AnnaMaria dresses and sandals. We're going to have Lieutenant Reed perform the ceremony; he's an ordained minister. We're going to

FURTHER INTO FIRE

have Pops give away AnnaMaria, and we're going to have Greek give away Melanie. All of 'B' shift from Station 7 is going to be there. What do you think?"

"I think you're the sweetest woman in the world."

"I was going to do it all and let you know about it after the fact, but since you insist you must know everything that goes on, there you have it."

First things first. When the girls were in school the next day, Kathleen went to see the manager of their apartment and told her what we were doing. There was always the chance that the manager was a homophobe, but thankfully it turned out that she adored the idea. Quickly, she and Kathleen went through the closet and looked at clothes sizes and ascertained that clothes were a size six and shoes were a size five. They left a notice on the cabinet that the maintenance crew had to look at the faucets, so if it were discovered anybody was inside it would alleviate a tiff. Kathleen came home, and the online shopping began. We spotted a gorgeous white eyelet skirt and peasant top for Melanie and a backless white halter dress with silver threads running through it for AnnaMaria. We got white sandals for Melanie and silver ones for AnnaMaria. I rented out the local civic center for two Saturdays from now, and Kathleen got on the phone and started calling all the people from her old firehouse. She also confirmed that Lt. Carl Reed was not going to be on vacation and would be available and willing to perform the services. The only part that couldn't be faked was the marriage certificate.

We had Celeste call Melanie and tell her there was one more thing that had come up, and she needed to get another copy of both her and AnnaMaria's driver's licenses and their birth certificates. They didn't question anything since Celeste had done so much for them. Melanie brought the documents over to our house, which I gave to Celeste the next day and returned to them the next night. Celeste used them to request a proxy application for a marriage license, and since Celeste was the attorney for both girls now, it was no problem. It got right down to the wire, but the license came in the mail on the Thursday prior to the big weekend. I'd already gotten Melanie and AnnaMaria to commit to the day at the civic center, telling them it was a party for Kevin.

When the girls got to the civic center, everybody else was already there. All the firefighters were there with their wives, and all of them were in their dress uniforms, which surprised the girls. All the firefighters' wives were wearing dresses or dressy pants, no jeans, and their children were spiffed up. Even Kathleen was wearing her departmental dress uniform. Martha and I were wearing dresses, and

Pops was in his dress policeman's uniform. At the front of the room, a table had been turned sideways and was adorned with flowers and ribbons. In the center of the table stood a pretty wooden cross.

"Oh, my gosh! I didn't know we were supposed to dress up. I feel so out of place!" said AnnaMaria.

"Do we have time to run back home and change?" asked Melanie.

"No, you're fine. Come here. I want you to meet everybody."

Kathleen introduced them to Mike Capcheczi, Greek, Dave, Stew, Scotty, Oliver, John, and Chris. Then, she introduced Carl Reed, who was both the lieutenant and the chaplain. Finally, she introduced all the wives and children. You could really tell that the girls felt out of place. Then Mike's wife, Estefanía took AnnaMaria by the hand and took her to one of the small rooms off to the side at the front of the hall, and Kathleen took Melanie to another room. Each room had a garment bag, a shoe box, and a bouquet of white miniature roses.

"I don't understand. What's going on?"

"Take off your clothes. Hurry up," Kathleen told Melanie.

"What?"

Kathleen unzipped the garment bag.

"Hurry up. Put these on," she said, holding up the skirt and blouse.

"I don't understand...."

"You don't have to understand, Cricket, just do it. If you don't take off your clothes, I'll do it for you. Just don't expect sex," she laughed with a snort.

Melanie turned around shyly, her back to Kathleen. As she took off her shirt, Kathleen handed her a camisole. After she put that on, Kathleen handed her the eyelet blouse.

"Now, drop the jeans, woman!" Kathleen laughed.

This time, Melanie had less apprehension and quickly shed her jeans. Kathleen handed her in order her half-slip, then her skirt. Next, the shoe box was brought out. Melanie oohed and aahed over the sandals. She didn't have to be told to put them on. She quickly buckled them into place. It was then, as she stared at the flowers on the table, the wheels began to quickly turn in her head. She looked at the flowers, then at Kathleen, then back at the flowers...back and forth. She launched herself at Kathleen, finally figuring out the plan for the day.

"Oh, Kathleen, you're so good to us! How can we ever thank you enough?" she blurted out, nearly strangling Kathleen, she was hugging her so tightly around the neck.

"Wait here, and let me check on AnnaMaria," Kathleen said with a chuckle.

Just then, there was a slight knock on the door, and Estefanía stuck her head in.

"Everybody ready here?"

"As ready as can be."

"Okay. Leave the door open and wait for the music. Greek is going to walk you down the aisle, and Pops is going to walk AnnaMaria. Good luck, Melanie."

"Thank you!"

As Estefanía moved out of the doorway, Greek's hulking but gentle frame showed up, nearly hitting the top of the door frame. The French horns began playing a trumpet voluntary indicating it was time for the ceremony to begin. When we were out in the hall and AnnaMaria and Melanie saw each other, Melanie scrunched up her shoulders and nose, smiling at AnnaMaria and waving to her. Kathleen's little Cricket had gone from a crude and crass, young, belligerent kid to a refined and sweet, young woman. She was so proud of her.

Kathleen and Scott took a lot of pictures of the affair. I was in the front row with little Kevin, who didn't make a fuss the whole time. He just cooed and looked around, still not able to focus on things in the distance, but he kept himself entertained, and I was happy at that. I wasn't sure how it would go. We had a real Minnesota reception: beer boiled brats to eat, beer for the adults, sodas for Melanie and the kids and one of the wives that was pregnant, and some hotdogs and a few burgers. All in all, everybody was extremely happy. I think the biggest surprise of all was the fact that somehow Kathleen had managed to get the ring sizes out of AnnaMaria one night at dinner and bought wedding rings that matched their engagement rings at Edgars'.

"So, AnnaMaria, we didn't mean to overstep our bounds. You haven't signed your marriage certificate yet. You could just refuse and decide you don't want to be married," I grinned.

Melanie and AnnaMaria were holding hands.

"Are you totally frickin' stupid? This is the most mind-blowing thing I've ever heard of. You didn't do this just to get in my pants, did you?" AnnaMaria laughed.

"Yes, as a matter of fact I did. Will you have my baby?" I laughed back.

"You two are something else."

"This was all Kathleen. It was totally her idea. We did some of the planning together, but it was all her. And I'll tell you this...You see all these people here? You're now a part of this family. Each and every one of them would lay down their lives for you both. If you ever needed something, you could call any one of them. I'm going to make sure you get everybody's email, so you can send them a thank you note."

"We do want their emails, but I also want their addresses. I want to write out a long thank you note and send it through snail mail."

"Will do."

After everybody had eaten just about all the food and drink they could handle, they migrated to the gifts table. Squeals of delight could be heard over and over again as the girls ripped through the wrapping paper.

"It's so amazing! Every single gift was exactly what we needed!" Melanie told Kathleen.

"Of course."

"How did everybody know?"

"Because I broke into your apartment."

"You what?"

"I told your landlady what I was up to. She thought it was wonderful. I was hesitant at first. I was afraid she might be a little homophobic bitch like your aunt, and did not know that you two were girlfriends, but she was in on it from the word go. We checked your clothes and shoe sizes. We checked out your apartment and kitchen. The whole gig. I figured, what the hell. We're family anyway, right?"

"You rat! You invaded our privacy!" snickered Melanie.

"Look, I've seen you naked before. What could be more private than that?"

Melanie punched Kathleen in the stomach and I laughed so hard I thought she was going to get hiccups. AnnaMaria just smiled the whole time, her arm intertwined with Melanie's.

"Do you know who this is?" asked AnnaMaria.

"Uh, Melanie?" I answered.

"No, it's my *wife*, Melanie!" she retorted with a blissful smile.

Kathleen and Scott and Oliver helped load all the presents into Melanie and AnnaMaria's car, then the entire gaggle of us gave them hugs and kisses, and we sent them on their way. All in all, it was a huge success.

"Speaking of wives, would you care to take me and your son home, my lovely wife?" I directed toward Kathleen.

"I'd love nothing more," she said.

❀ ❀ ❀

Kevin was crawling in his playpen one day and ran into the mesh. He was confused that he'd run out of room, little goof. He started grunting and squawking and carrying on like nobody's business. I turned him around, and he crawled to the other side, running into the mesh again, prompting more noises and frustration. This time, instead of just turning him around, I pulled him gently by his arm until he pretty much crawled in a circle. It's almost like you could smell the sawdust burning in his little head. He paused for the longest time, then he took off like a rabbit for the other side. This time, when he hit the wall, he simply turned and ran to the other side, the whole time laughing like he'd discovered the world's most intensely amazing game. I'll have to say, motherhood is the greatest thing. Well, maybe tied to the married thing. It was definitely enhanced by Kathleen being up in the evenings before work and the two of us playing with Kevin. Many nights, Pops and Martha were over, or AnnaMaria and Melanie, although they couldn't ever stay too long because of their homework from nursing school.

"Bel, I need to talk to you about something," Kathleen broached one evening when Kevin was three months old.

"Uh-oh, this sounds ominous."

"No, I just don't want to catch a ration of shit from you, that's all."

"What is it, baby?"

"I want to have Kevin christened."

You could have heard a pin drop.

"Where did this come from? I thought you didn't do the Catholic thing anymore, other than midnight mass on Christmas."

"I've just been thinking about it lately. I want Mike and Estefanía to be his godparents."

"I've got no problem with that, if that's what you want."

"It is what I want. Don't ask me why."

"Have you asked them yet?" I asked.

"Of course not! Didn't I promise to talk to you first on everything from now on?"

"Well, well, well. You're officially pussy whipped!"

"Don't let it get out, okay? My friends will make fun of me."

"Oh, Kathleen, I hate to burst your bubble, but your friends already make fun of you, just about as much as you make fun of them!"

We cuddled up against each other on the couch, cradling Kevin between us while he played with the buttons on Kathleen's uniform until she had to head to work.

I had just finished nursing and burping Kevin when my phone chirped, notifying me that I had a text.

'Guess what? The masked man has struck again.'

'What in the world are you talking about?'

'I got into the station, and there was a manila envelope marked Bella Pope.'

'That's funny. Open it up and tell me what the shots are.'

'No way. I'll bring it home tomorrow morning and you can open it. It's addressed to you.'

'Don't be stupid. Just open it.'

'Wouldn't dream of it. Anyway, I have to hit the streets. When I went on fires it was hit or miss. With Medic it's almost non-stop. We have waits here and there, like after we hit the hospital, but we have lots of runs. I'll see you later, sweetie. Sweet dreams.'

'You be safe out there, baby.'

'Spare the rod and spoil the child.'

'How dare you!'

'lol'

One thing about Kevin, at three months, he was already sleeping all the way through the night. That alone was worth its weight in gold. And I was, with Kathleen's help and guidance, losing my baby fat. I was never built like Kathleen—no abs, no biceps, no quads—but I'd had a flat stomach and had been thin my whole life. I knew I couldn't ever get my hips back in place, even with a vice, but I wanted my stomach back and at least most of the fat gone from my thighs. I loved the fact that Kathleen loved kissing my thighs and running her hands up and down them and all over my tummy, but at the same time I hated it and was always self-conscious about it. Just thinking about it, I heaved a huge sigh and gathered Kevin in my arms, taking him upstairs with me. I changed him and put him in his PJs, then got my own on and climbed between the sheets. I was out like a light in seconds.

Kathleen waited until about nine o'clock to call Mike.

"Hey, brother. You fighting any fires today?"

"Not yet. How's that new baby of yours doing?"

"He's doing so great. Say, that's why I'm calling you. If something happened to me and Bella, would you promise to bring up Kevin as a Catholic?"

"What in the hell are you talking about? You're acting a little crazy!"

"We're going to get him christened, and we want you and Estefanía to be his godparents. That is, if you want to."

"Well, hell yeah! I can't think of a greater honor! And besides, if you and Bella did die in a car wreck or something, one more mouth to feed with our four wouldn't make a hill of beans difference!"

"Hey, Mikey. Your filter's broken again."

They both laughed long and hard at that.

"Just let me know where and when, and we'll round up the family and all be there. Oops, speaking of fires, there goes the alarm. Gotta run."

"Yeah, I can hear. Be careful out there, rookie."

FURTHER INTO FIRE

"I got your rookie hanging, medic!"

"Hey, baby. What's up?" I answered the phone.

"I just talked to Mike and...Shit! That's us. Got to roll the bus. Call you later," Kathleen said as she clicked off before I got an answer.

Such was life being married to an emergency responder, be it fire or rescue.

❊ ❊ ❊

Kathleen and her partner, Camden, were parked in the lot at Wendy's, eating lunch, when their radio started squawking.

"Medic 8, please respond to shots fired at the Gas and Go on Jackson Street. Officer down and one possible DOA. Medic 4 also dispatched."

"Dispatch, Medic 8 responding. We'll be on site in three minutes," Cammie responded.

Kathleen and Cammie were two peas in a pod. Both were hard-working, dedicated, and selfless, and both worked out constantly. Cammie and her husband had two children in elementary school. They'd been to our house several times for dinner and we'd been to their house. We couldn't wait until late spring when we could move outside for barbecues.

Medic 8 was first on scene and found the police officer sitting on the floor, his back up against the pay counter and his arms crossed over his chest, wincing.

"*Pops!* What in the hell did you go and get yourself into?" Kathleen screamed as she ran to him, just as Medic 4's siren could be heard pulling in.

"Well, Kitten, I think I just happened to be in the wrong place at the wrong time. I'm okay, though. I just took a couple rounds to my vest. It's just the pressure shock that's causing me some pain. Go back down the second aisle and check on the perp. Go carefully, though. I'm ninety-nine point nine percent sure that he's dead, but just the same, you can't be too careful!" whispered Pops, obviously in more pain than he would admit.

"Hey, Jason. Take care of my dad here, will you? I think he just took a couple of rounds to his vest. Get it off and make sure there isn't any subdural damage and the bullets didn't pierce it. I'm going to go back here and check out this other guy."

"I'm on it, rookie."

"Yeah, and you can tell Mike to shove it up his ass!" Kathleen laughed over her shoulder to the message obviously delivered by her earlier conversation with Mike. She moved to the back of the store, cautiously stepping back slowly, keeping her eyes open for any movement from the assailant.

When she got to him, there was nothing to check. He had two entry wounds to his face: one through his lower jaw and one through his nose. Nobody said criminals were smart. Even knowing that police officers wear armored vests, they get scared and just aim for the body. Police are trained to aim for head shots where they are almost guaranteed certain stopping power…lethal stopping power. Kathleen leaned down over the body and checked his carotid artery for a pulse and found none, just as she suspected. There was little blood on the floor as the bullets had not exited from the skull. This was no longer a job for a medic. It was a job for Crime Scene Investigation. Kathleen walked back to the front of the store, where she found that Pops had already been moved.

She walked around to the back of Medic 4's ambulance, where the doors were open. Pops was sitting on the floor, his feet hanging off the back, talking to Jason and Joseph, the two paramedics for that team. They were talking about fly fishing up in the north woods. Pops had his vest and shirt off. He already had a pretty good bruise from one of the slugs but none from the other.

"Oh, hi, Kitten. Did you see what that jackass did to my vest? It'll cost me six hundred bucks to get this replaced. Six hundred bucks! Do you think the department is going to pay for this?" he said holding up his Point Blank performance vest.

"You'd rather you hadn't worn it today? Maybe left it hanging in the closet, so it would stay nice and clean, free of rips and tears?" Kathleen laughed at him.

"That's not the point! Stupid punk chose this morning to rob the store! All I wanted was a couple of apple fritters for your mom!" he gruffed.

"Pops, you're just a big goof. Did you hear yourself?" she asked, ruffling up his hair.

"What's that?"

"You didn't say Martha. You called her my mother."

"Hey, I did, didn't I? Well, I've got to say, Kitten, you are one cool cat! You waltz in here, seemingly without a care, and just do your business. I'll give you that."

"You have no idea. You scared the living shit out of me at first. Until I knew that you were okay, all I could think about was living without you, and how terrible it would be for me…for the whole family…everyone."

"Well, I'm all right, so you don't have to worry about anything. Just promise me one thing: Don't tell Martha."

"Oh, you have to tell Martha!"

"I will as soon as I get home. I just want to be there in person to show her I'm doing just fine. I don't want her to hear it from somebody else and have her start worrying over nothing. Got it?"

"Yeah, Pops. I got it. See you soon. Love you."

"I love you too, Kitten."

He tried to hug her, but the bruising made it a bit difficult.

"Get my Pops a blanket will ya, guys? It's cold out! See you later, Jason. Joseph."

Both Kathleen and Camden got back in their ambulance and let dispatch know they were waiting for CSI to give their statements. They were waiting onsite in the meanwhile. They finished their now cold chicken bites and French fries listening to the radio.

※ ※ ※

I was looking for a letter that I'd gotten from HR about my time on short-term disability with Kevin when I'd been at home for three months. I searched the office, the living room, our bedroom…everywhere. Just on a lark, I went into the kitchen and pulled the trash out from under the sink. Maybe I'd thrown it away accidentally? I did find it in the trash can, a little damp but none the worse for wear. But just under that, I found an envelope with the return address from the State of Minnesota, Department of the Highway Patrol. It was a Saturday afternoon, and Kathleen was on duty that late June day. Kevin was just a little over seven months old. I was tempted to leave the letter there, but I couldn't resist. I picked it up, guiltily.

'Dear Mrs. Pope,

We are happy to inform you that you have been selected to rejoin our helicopter rescue team. Please bring your driver's license, your birth certificate, and a current valid flight certificate to our headquarters, and we will begin your in-processing.

Our entire department appreciates the hardships that you have had to endure with your previous accident while on duty within our department, and we could not be happier that you are now well enough to return to our active roster. We will hold your position open until July 10th.

Thank you for your consideration,

Major Thomson Riddle,

Chief, Air Operations.'

I was stunned. I had no idea what to think. Thousands of thoughts ran through my head. The more I thought about it, the more I was convinced that Kathleen couldn't pass a flight physical and thus couldn't fly. I wasn't sure whether to leave it buried in the trash or what. I steeled myself and wiped the letter down, drying it thoroughly.

As I walked upstairs to put it in my nightstand, Kevin was doing his favorite new trick. He was standing up in the playpen, bouncing up and down on his legs, holding onto the top rail, saying, 'bah bah bah bah bah bah bah' and slobbering everywhere. He was a pretty cute kid. Although I'd wanted children, I had no idea how much I would enjoy them until I had given birth to Kevin. And I think the same could be said for Kathleen. On days we both worked we had a nanny come to the house. On days when she was off and I worked, she stayed home and played Mom. Actually, that's a lie. They went out to show off almost every day—to the park, or the zoo, or the nursing home where Kathleen read to the elderly. She also went over to Martha's to visit at least twice a week.

Kathleen got home after getting off shift around forty minutes after midnight. I was sitting up in bed reading a book. She went into Kevin's room first to check him, kiss him, and watch him sleep for a few minutes. Then, she came into the bedroom.

"Hey, sweetie. How are you tonight?"

I didn't answer, just kept on reading.

"Bella? Hello?"

I held my book in place and just looked up over the top of my reading glasses, not quite glaring.

"Okay, so you want to tell me what's going on or what I've done, since it's one of those looks?" Kathleen asked.

"What makes you think you've done anything?" I handed back to her, completely deadpan.

"Well, in addition to the look, that answer," she sighed, dropping her shoulders, getting the message loud and clear that I was definitely not happy.

I closed the book and set it down. Then, I reached into the nightstand and pulled out the letter from the highway patrol.

"Kathleen, is it that you don't think you can pass a flight physical? Why don't you go and try? At least that way you will have tried. What have you got to lose?"

"Oh, so now you're snooping in the trash after me," she asked defensively.

"No, I accidentally threw away something from HR that was really important, and it was just under that. I wasn't snooping at all. I would never do that. But this is not about me. It's about you."

"For your information, I've already passed a flight physical. I did it about a month ago."

FURTHER INTO FIRE

I couldn't think what to say next. My jaw just dropped open.

"You're not saying anything now, are you?"

"Kathleen, for goodness sake! Why didn't you tell me?"

"Because it wasn't any big deal."

"But you could get a job on LifeFlight at least. And now this? I mean, are you just throwing this letter away and you're taking the job? You are, of course, going to take the job, aren't you? It's your dream job!"

"I've been thinking about it."

"What's there to think about? Next week, march your little red fanny down there and put in your paperwork, damn it!"

"That's not very ladylike, y'know?"

"Kathleen, this isn't a laughing matter. And you know, I'm not in a very laughing mood that you didn't tell me about this either. You *promised* me you would discuss this kind of thing with me."

"Well, here's the thing: I've been mulling this thing over and talking to Camden on shift–"

"Oh, so you'll talk to your new girlfriend, but you won't talk to me. Is that it?" I stared at her with an icy glare.

"What? You're sounding a little crazy here. I wasn't talking to her about *me*, I was talking to her about *her* and her long-term plans: Sticking it out with St. Paul or going private. Whether she'd ever considered LifeFlight or anything like that."

"Oh. Well...."

"Do you ever get jealous over Cammie?"

"Once in a while. I mean, she's pretty, you ride around together every third day...all day...."

"Aww, that's so cute. You do know she's totally straight, married, and has two kids, right?"

"Yes, but when my head starts spinning, all that doesn't matter."

"Somebody's still got some postpartum depression going on in her cute little head!" she said, mussing my hair.

"Maybe. Just leave me alone! And I'd really appreciate it if you'd talk to me!"

"Okay, here's the thirty-second spiel. I'm not going back to work for them. I'm staying here in St. Paul. I like what I'm doing. I like the type of shifts I work, and I have for most of the last nine years of my life. I like the fact that I am still a firefighter and will occasionally get the opportunity to work in that capacity, still get training, and still keep my certification. And for your information, I opened that letter after you went to bed last night. You had a headache and went to bed at nine o'clock. I was going to tell you as soon as I got home. So there."

I drew Kathleen deeply into my arms and hugged her tightly with tears running down my cheeks. I felt happy that she wanted to work for St. Paul. I felt bad that I had treated her a bit roughly. I felt sad that she'd given up her dream of flying because I knew she totally loved that. I was chock full of emotions, and she was right: I was battling postpartum doldrums. She fixed that though. She took off her uniform and underwear, then removed my pajamas. Then she laid down with her head at the foot of the bed and mine at the head of the bed, and we began to simultaneously burrow ourselves into each other's pleasure centers until our worlds rocked.

As we were under the sheet holding each other, Kathleen stroking my shoulder, she turned to speak to me.

"I will tell you this. I am going to do something this coming fall. It's going to be a surprise. It's going to be a huge deal. And I'm not going to consult you on it. So, as much as you want me to let you in on everything, this one time I'm not going to. But I'm letting you know there is a thing, so that at least you know there is a thing. I know that's vague, but you'll find out about it eventually, and you'll go, 'Aha, that was the thing!' and this way it won't be like it was totally behind your back. Can I at least get away with this one thing?" Kathleen asked.

"I dare you to diagram that sentence," I said, laughing.

"Well? Do I have your permission?"

I thought about it for about five minutes.

"Well, I can't think what it could possibly be, but for this single instance, Kathleen Marie Pope, I give you my specific permission to bend the rules since you've at least admitted that there is a 'thing.'"

"You're the best, sweetie."

"You're damned right I am. Go get Kevin and bring him in here with us tonight."

"I don't think so."

"Why not? One night won't break his routine."

"Because I'm not finished with you yet," Kathleen said with an evil grin.

❦ ❦ ❦

The next morning, on a Sunday, Kathleen called Mike Capcheczi about nine thirty.

"Hey, Mike. You guys going to mass this morning?"

"We were, but two of the kids have a fever, so we're just going to hang around here."

"What are the chances that Nana can hang with the kids, and you and Estefanía can meet me somewhere for lunch around eleven thirty? I need a nice, quiet sit-down with just the two of you; nobody else present. Somewhere out of the way, not a busy place."

"Go to Leo's. We'll be there. Eleven thirty, right?"

"Yup. Got it. See you then."

Kathleen pulled into the parking lot at eleven ten and went inside. She told the waitress there would be two others joining her and ordered some iced tea. She hadn't been sitting down for five minutes when Mike and Estefanía walked up to the table. They order fried mushrooms for starters and just talked for a bit about kids and life. When they were done with the mushrooms, they ordered brats and onion rings all around.

"You know I had a lot of internal damage from my crash, right?" asked Kathleen

Both Mike and Estefanía shook their heads.

"The thing is, they had to remove my right ovary, but I still have my left one. They had to take a couple of nicks from my uterus and put in the odd stitch, but not too much. They said it would 'probably' still work, but no guarantees because there was some heavy bruising. No way to tell, unless it just plain doesn't work. Maybe my eggs work, but won't implant properly," Kathleen said as she paused, heaving a huge sigh.

"And I take it this is the reason you've called us to today's little meeting?" asked Mike.

"Yessir. We went to the fertility clinic for Bella. Worked first time. Apparently, she's pretty fertile. With me, it will probably be a little harder. They may have to implant several times, and even then, there's no money back warranty."

"Okay. We get it," Mike said, taking Estefanía's hand in his, "and you needed somebody you could trust to talk to about this?" he asked.

"Not exactly. Now, here's the thing," Kathleen said, laughing nervously.

She started playing with her napkin, looking down at the table.

"You need a donor, right?" quizzed Estefanía.

Kathleen said nothing, just kept playing with her napkin, looking down at the table, nodding her head in assent.

"I, for one, have no problem with Mike going to the clinic and giving the specimen, if that's what you're asking. I think that would be a noble thing to do!" exclaimed Estefanía without even waiting for Mike to respond.

"Are you sure, honey?" Mike asked his wife.

"Of course. She's family. You'd do it for your sister or one of mine, wouldn't you? What's the difference? I know we're about ten years older than Kathleen, but I mean, shit, we've known her since she was a teenager, for God's sake. Kathleen? What are you going to do if it doesn't take?"

"I guess we'll get Bella pregnant again, and that will just be the way it is. I don't have a problem with that. If that's the way it's got to be, then that's life. It's not going to kill me if I can't carry. And it's funny, before Bella got pregnant I never thought I'd want to have a baby of my own. It was never an option with any of my previous partners."

"Speaking of your previous partners, it's really great how Melanie's turned out. Her problem wasn't that she was a bad girl, she was just young and totally scared, I think. I'm really glad that you two have ended up being good friends," said Mike.

"Me and you both. I totally agree. We have them over all the time for dinner. They're both in nursing school right now, and they'll finish in about another year and a half or so. They play with Kevin all the time. They love him just like they're his aunties. It's too funny," laughed Kathleen.

"Kathleen, I want to tell you something else. If you don't get an implant to take, and I don't say this lightly, I'll take your eggs and be your surrogate. No joke. I'll do that for you."

"Estefanía, that's so sweet of you, but let's cross that bridge when we get to it. Okay?" Kathleen said, squeezing her hand.

Kathleen gave them the name of the clinic, and Mike went down later that week and gave his donation, leaving instructions that it was to be used solely for Kathleen Pope. Kathleen went in the following week to start getting the hormone shots for receptivity, and six weeks later, she got her first implant. After four weeks, she'd gone back to the clinic to find out they'd not attached to her uterus. As heartbroken as she was, she started the hormone therapy again, and eight weeks later, she was ready for the second implant attempt.

❦ ❦ ❦

In mid-December, on one of her days off, Kathleen called Martha after first arranging for the nanny to work an extra day.

"Hi, Martha. I need you to go to the doctor's office with me this morning. Appointment's at eleven fifteen. Can you make it?"

"Sure. Who are you going to see?" Martha asked.

"Dr. Scott, my OB/GYN."

"Are you having a problem or something?"

"Or something. Drive over here early, and we'll have a cup of coffee before we go. Frieda will be here taking care of Kevin. I'm just asking her to work an extra half day."

"I'll be there in about half an hour."

Kathleen hadn't told anybody that she'd already been back to the fertility clinic eight times for checkups since the initial implanting of the fertilized eggs. She never believed in a million years it would work, but the second attempt had yielded success, and here she was going for her first ultrasound. She didn't tell Martha what the visit was for; she'd figured on surprising her. They waited approximately forty-five minutes outside in the waiting area, then were taken to an exam room where they waited another thirty.

"I'm sorry, Mrs. Pope, that we're so backed up today. It's been an absolute mad house in here!" said Laci, the nurse.

"Don't sweat it. We don't have anywhere else to be."

Laci took Kathleen's vitals, checked her medications list, listened to her heart, asked her if she was taking her vitamins, and then asked her the date of her last period. Martha didn't pick up on the questions. She knew that Kathleen had been in the horrific helicopter crash and assumed she was having some problems related to that. Then, the nurse smiled and put her pen in her pocket.

"Okay, Mrs. Pope, if you'd follow me into the lab," holding her hand out, indicating she should follow.

Martha just sat in her chair, assuming Kathleen was going for a blood draw.

"Martha, come on. Don't just sit there like a bump on a log!"

Martha picked up her purse and quickly pulled up the rear of the little train of people moving down the hall and filing into the ultrasound room. Laci had Kathleen lay back on the exam table, telling her the technician would be in very soon.

"What are they looking for, Kathleen? What sort of problem do they think you have?"

"Just wait and see. It won't be long now."

Martha took a chair to one side of the exam table as Kathleen got up on the table, pulling her shirt up high around her waist and tucking a bit of it in under the bottom cuff of her sports bra to hold it in place, and waited for the technician. The technician came in about ten minutes later, and looked at Martha.

"Oh, hi, Mrs. Pope. How's your grandson? Well, I hope?"

"Hi, Tori. Yes, fine, fine. Kathleen, this is the young lady who did the ultrasounds for Bella. Tori, this is my daughter, Kathleen."

"Hi, Kathleen. Pleasure to meet you. How far along are you?"

"I think about eight weeks."

Martha's eyes glazed over. She didn't move a muscle for the longest time. Tori fired up the ultrasound machine, asked Kathleen to pull her sweat pants down a few inches, and squirted goop all over her. Martha still hadn't budged. Her mouth was only slightly open, and she hadn't even blinked in all this time.

Tori had begun moving all around just doing the initial scan. She kept saying 'Hmm' over and over.

"Okay, okay, enough of the 'hmms.' What are you finding? What's wrong?" Kathleen asked in alarm.

"There's nothing wrong. Just lay back and relax, Kathleen."

The thought of something wrong finally got Martha moving again.

"Have you found something? Is there something wrong with my daughter?"

"I wouldn't say wrong. I also wouldn't say that unusual these days. A bit abnormal maybe," chuckled Tori.

"*What?*" cried out Martha and Kathleen in unison.

"Well, you see this here? This is over a bit on the right-hand side. For the moment, we'll call this baby A, and over here, see? This is farther left and a little higher, and we'll call this baby B."

"Are you sure there are only two? From what I understood they only implanted two at a time because they thought the odds of them taking weren't that good. And neither of them took the first attempt," stated Kathleen.

"Kathleen? You had…I mean…You? You're?" Martha said, her hand half over her mouth with a smile that was getting bigger and bigger by the moment.

"Yeah, ain't it a kick? I didn't want to say anything to anybody until now. The chances were just too high that I'd have an ectopic pregnancy or a spontaneous abortion due to the crash last spring. Kevin's going to have a couple of playmates. What do you think?"

Martha started wailing and carrying on and hugging Kathleen.

"Did you do this with Bella?" Kathleen asked.

"Yes, pretty much. About the same," she said, wiping her tears and jumping up and down a little bit.

"Ladies, if it's not too much to ask, can I get back to my job here?" laughed Tori.

She went back to work and the general scans. She got the babies turned just right. One was a boy and one was a girl. It was usually hard to tell so early, but the twins were very cooperative. That made Kathleen so very, very happy. Tori took snapshots of each showing their respective sexes. Then, she went to each baby and started taking measurements and recording all the data. She handed Kathleen a towel to clean up with and handed them a stack of about ten photos of each of the baby's ultrasounds.

As soon as they were out of the doctor's office, Kathleen called Pops.

"Hey, Kitten. What's up?"

"Be at our place for dinner tonight at seven o'clock. Martha's spending the day with me, so she'll already be there. We're having a pot roast."

"Sounds good. I'll be there."

"Love you, Pops."

"Love you too, Kitten."

The next call she made was to me.

"Hi, baby. You having fun on your day off? How's my baby boy?"

"Wouldn't know. Martha and I are out. I had the nanny come over for half a day, but we're going to go by the store for a pot roast and some things. We're going to have Pops come over tonight, so we can all have dinner together. Make sure you're home at six. Okay?"

"No problem. It's a normal day," I replied, wondering what had gotten into her bonnet.

After the first two calls, Kathleen called Mike.

"Hello?"

"Estefanía, you guys got any plans for tonight?"

"Nope. Just a regular school night. Why?"

"You guys have it easy with Mike's mom living with you; built-in babysitting."

"Where did that come from?"

"Have Nana babysit tonight. Be at our place at seven and eat dinner with us. It's sort of important."

"Okay. Mike's over with Greek right now doing something in his garage, but I'll call him. See you tonight."

"Bye."

The last call she made was to Melanie and AnnaMaria.

"Hi, Kathleen."

"Hi, Cricket. Listen, start your homework early. I need you over here for dinner at seven sharp. Got it?"

"Sounds ominous."

"Yes, it is. But in a good way."

"Cool. We'll be there."

"Don't be late. I'd hate to have to give you a spanking!"

"Ooo…Do you promise?"

"You wish!"

"I think my wife would be mad. Unless maybe you gave her one too!"

Kathleen could hear AnnaMaria giggling in the background.

"Are you two always joined at the wrist by a six-inch piece of string?" Kathleen snorted.

"Pretty much. See you guys tonight!"

※ ※ ※

When I got home about five-fifteen, Martha was sitting in the easy chair. The playpen was folded up in the corner, and Kathleen was guarding the entry to the kitchen. Kevin had free range of the whole floor. Of course, the gates were put up at both sets of stairs and at the office. He was jetting around like a rocket these days. At eleven months old, he was walking. Sometimes he reverted to crawling though, and when he did he was like a greyhound out of the gate at Pimlico, but for the most part he walked around and held onto things here and there. I scooped him up into my arms after I dropped my coat and boots.

"How's Mama's big boy?" I asked him, showering him with kisses.

That always made him laugh, unless he was trying to eat, and then, it irritated the living daylights out of him. He'd already learned to call both Kathleen and I 'Ma.' We kept trying to get him to say, 'Mama K' and 'Mama B,' but so far, no luck. He did know 'Pop' and 'Marf' though. And he called both Melanie and AnnaMaria 'Mel.' I would keep trying.

"What's so important that we have a strict dinner hour?" I asked.

"We have guests."

"Who?"

"People."

"Your parents?"

"And others."

"Care to say who?"

"Not yet. Oh, and we're having blackened chicken and red beans instead of pot roast."

"Whatever."

I walked over to Kathleen. Still holding Kevin in one arm, I sat down on the floor in front of Kathleen. I put the back of my hand on her forehead.

"Are you feeling okay?" I asked.

"Never better."

"Okay, stop. You're acting just plain spooky. What gives? Spill it."

"We'll talk at dinner. Go get changed into something comfy. Hey, Martha. Would you mind if I went upstairs and had sex with my wife?"

"No, go ahead. I'll watch Kevin."

"Will you *please* stop embarrassing me all the time? Well, that was a stupid question. Like after four years that's going to change!" I laughed.

I'd just come back downstairs when Mike and Estefanía knocked on the door. One of the nice things we'd done to our house last year was to double the width of the driveway. We still had a single car garage, but we poured a completely new driveway, so that it wasn't full of cracks and crevices, and in doing so made it a two-car width.

"Hi, guys. What are you doing here tonight?" I asked.

"We ran out of beer, and we thought you might have some." Mike snickered.

"And it wouldn't have been cheaper to get some at the store rather than drive all the way over here?" I ventured.

"Yeah, it is about dinner time, and we thought maybe we might scam some free food too," said Estefanía.

"Well, come on in. We're having blackened chicken and beans. We have enough for everyone, baby?" I called out to Kathleen.

"Oh, yeah. There's enough for a small army tonight; there's still more people coming over."

"How many more?" I asked, sort of puzzled why people were coming over during the week.

"Just a few."

"How many is a few?"

"Three."

"Which three?"

"Guess."

"Pops...."

"Yup."

"Who else?"

"You'll see."

About thirty minutes later, the doorbell rang again. I opened the door, and it was the girls. Pops was standing right behind them. Everybody came in and took their coats and boots off. With the place beginning to fill up, I set the playpen back up and hoisted Kevin over the side.

"Whoa, there. Bring my little man over here to me," hollered Pops.

I don't think there'd ever been a prouder grandpa. And naming Kevin after him, even though his middle name was my dad's? Oh, it just added fodder to the fire.

"Everybody sit down, and let me check on dinner," said Kathleen.

I heard the oven door open, then shut. Kathleen came back in. Mike, Estefanía, Martha, and I already had a beer. Kathleen brought in two more, one for AnnaMaria and one for Pops, as well as an iced tea for Melanie.

"What about a beer for you, baby?" I asked tenderly, holding Kathleen's hand.

"I've got an iced tea in here on the counter. I'm good."

"Do you feel sick or something?"

"No, I told you, I feel great."

"I think the last time you turned down a beer was...*Never!*"

"I'm good. Now, go in the other room," Kathleen said, placing a kiss on my forehead.

Everybody was talking in twos and threes when Kathleen came in and took Kevin from Pops and put him back into the playpen.

"Martha, may I have the envelope please?" Kathleen said with no small amount of flourish.

Martha opened her purse and brought out a small manila envelope, handing it to Kathleen. I was sitting in the easy chair now. Everybody else was sitting on the couch or chairs we'd brought in from the kitchen. Kathleen walked over in front of me and knelt in front of me.

"Do you remember a few months ago? I told you I was going to do something and not talk to you about it?"

"Vaguely. I hadn't really thought about it for a while."

"Well, I've done it. And now, it's time to...uh...confess my sins, as it were."

"Are you contrite? Do you have sorrow in your heart for committing this sin?" I asked, jokingly.

"Actually, no. Now, the question is whether I get to sleep in bed with you tonight in our house, or do I have to go home with one of our guests tonight and seek asylum?"

"Okay, now you're just starting to scare me. You've had a weird look on your face since you've been home. You're not drinking a beer like every single other person here tonight... Oh, my *God!* Kathleen Marie! Don't tell me!" I yelled at the top of my voice.

Kathleen extracted the two photos from the envelope that showed the two babies and their gender.

"I give you baby A, tentatively named Madeline, and baby B, tentatively named Michael," she said, handing them over to me.

"Kathleen Marie! What have you *done?*" I shouted again.

"I think, more to the point, it's what we've done. And before you go getting totally bent out of shape, it's something that I never thought would happen. And it took twice. Shutting up about it has been the hardest thing I've ever done in my life. Quite frankly, the doctor at the fertility clinic didn't give me much hope. And then, when I got pregnant, he told me not to keep my hopes up that they would make it to the eight-week point. That's why I did things the way I did. Do you forgive me?"

I just kept staring at the two pictures, back and forth, from one to the other.

"Oh, I get it. I have one, so you have to go and have two. Is that it? You always have to go one better than everybody else. You are so damn competitive!" I said, trying to keep a straight face.

"No, that's not it. They did two eggs at a time, thinking that I'd be lucky to get one to attach. I mean–"

"And what are all these people here for? Your posse? You too afraid to face me yourself? Is that it?" I yelled, still leaning farther and farther forward in my chair, seconds away from losing my mad face any second.

"No, Pops is here because I wanted him to know. Martha was with me at the doctor's today, and I thought it would be something that Melanie and AnnaMaria would want to know about, since they love Kevin so much, and–"

"And Mike? What about Mike? What's he doing here?"

Then my mouth dropped open and my hand halfway pointed to him and Estefanía. Mike was sitting on one end of the couch with Estefanía sitting on the arm, leaning against him, her arm around him, both grinning like the Cheshire cat.

"He's…He's…the…."

"Uh, yeah, he is. I mean, he's in excellent physical shape, he's got a college degree, all four of their children are in gifted programs at school, and he's in excellent health. And here's the thing…If I'd gone three rounds and it hadn't worked, Estefanía had already offered to be a surrogate and carry my fertilized egg. Do you realize what a commitment they were willing to make for us? I just didn't want to jinx it or anything, if that makes sense. Would you talk to me? Say something. Say anything. Hit me if you want. Bella? Sweetie?"

I launched myself off the chair and onto Kathleen, knocking her backwards onto the floor. I started kissing her and hugging her, pulling her to me, and before I knew it, I couldn't stop cackling.

"We're pregnant again!" I squealed.

"Does this mean I'm not in the doghouse?" Kathleen asked, hesitantly.

"You never were. I was putting on an act, and I came very close to losing it, more than once. It was just too much fun! Oh, baby. This is such a good surprise. And you!" I said, jumping up from the floor, running over to Mike and Estefanía, wrapping an arm around each of them, swinging them back and forth.

"By the way, if you ever do that to me, CSI won't find enough pieces of you to identify the body!" AnnaMaria said to Melanie, making a point of everybody hearing it.

Everybody in the room heard her and laughed.

Kevin started jumping on his tiptoes and holding his arms up.

"Mama K. Up, up."

"Hey, that's the first time he's gotten it right!" I shouted as Kathleen raced over, picking him up in her arms and kissing him all over his face.

We all loaded up our plates and spread out around the living room. We ate and talked and laughed and smiled until about nine o'clock, when everybody started heading home. It was, after all, a school night.

※ ※ ※

We were on the North Shore with the kids for the weekend, taking photographs of the beautiful fall colors changing all around us. Kevin was five, and Maddy and Mikey were four. It was the perfect fall day. The skies were a deep, clear blue, and not a cloud was in sight. The temperature was sixty-two degrees, and we had a long, four-day weekend that we'd arranged to take off.

"Mom, is this where you cracked Mama B's head open like an egg?" Kevin asked with a grin on his face, holding Kathleen's hand, toe to toe at the very edge of the cliff.

Despite being the direct fruit of my womb, he was Kathleen's little protégé. Every chance he got to say or ask something to get a rise out of me, or anybody else for that matter, was considered a victory in his little eyes…his precocious little eyes. We were forever getting notes from his kindergarten teacher about such incidences. Never for anything bad, just things that probably shouldn't be brought up by children his age—and weren't brought up by any other children!

Then there were Maddy and Mikey. They were fraternal twins, but you wouldn't know it to observe their behavior. They did everything together. They played together at home all the time, always the same games and always the same toys. We had intentionally placed them in different preschool classes, hoping to give them some time to themselves, but before and after class, they immediately came together like magnets.

Maddie had gotten us summoned to a couple of parent-teacher conferences just a couple of weeks into the term. Apparently, she and Brenda Cargill struck up an immediate friendship on the first day of school. They played together, sat together, ate lunch together (it was an all-day class, as was Kevin's) and were inseparable on the playground, to the exclusion of all the other children. The day they reached the point of holding hands and kissing each other, was the day we met with the teacher, the principal, and Mr. and Mrs. Cargill.

"Are there any other children behaving this way?" asked Sam Cargill in the meeting.

"Well, we have one other pair of children," answered the principal.

"Are their parents being hauled in for counseling?" he asked, "or are we being singled out because our children are the same sex?"

"Well, we are talking to the children, telling them that this is not the appropriate place for such behavior."

"Are you afraid that Maddy is going to turn Bren-Bren into a lesbian like the Popes?"

"No, sir…" she started.

"We've already met them because of Bren and Maddy's friendship. We've had dinner with them twice. Did you know that Bella is a Fulbright scholar and she graduated at the age of twenty-four with a master's degree in business and economics, all the while working for over 18 months on internships? Did you know that Kathleen put herself through college working as a police dispatcher, then as a firefighter for St. Paul, during which time she studied for and successfully passed a paramedic's course and transitioned to that career for a living? Me? My parents footed my whole bill. Shit. If that's what it's like to be a lesbian, give me a transgender operation and let me fight the good fight. Now, if there's nothing further, it's getting close to dinner time and our families need to get together and feel a little loving! Good night, ma'am."

❧ ❧ ❧

Kathleen could tell by the look on my face that Kevin standing so close to the edge of the escarpment made me a bit nervous, so she started walking back toward the rest of us. I heaved a sigh of relief. Kevin was fearless. Every time he showed how fearless he was, the mother in me started having panic attacks and running through a thousand scenarios where he would be hurt and lying in a hospital with tubes running in and out of his little body. Silly, I know, but it was all part of being a mommy.

As usual, Mikey and Maddie were holding hands, squatting down, looking very carefully at small pebbles, and examining them to see which ones were worthy of taking home to add to their constantly growing collection. We always told them they could only bring home two each to put in their terrarium with the hermit crabs. They'd named them Molly and Maggie, for whatever reason, and we assured them that the crabs were indeed female, to keep them from asking too many questions for the moment.

It was lunch time, and we went back to the SUV to grab the ice chest and make sandwiches, eat some fruit, and pass out juice boxes.

"Mama B, can I see your stretch marks?" asked Kevin.

"Oh, you know I hate that Kevin! Why do you ask that?" I questioned with a fury in my voice.

"Because I know it makes you mad. I know it's because I was inside you and I was so big," he said with a giggle.

"You know, you did this to me, you bitch!" I directed at Kathleen.

"Aha! Dollar for the swear jar!" laughed Kevin.

I'd been had. I knew he did it on purpose, that I'd been baited. I couldn't help but laugh. He was definitely not my child. He was Kathleen through and through. The funny thing was that both of Kathleen's biological children were more mine. They always came to me before Kathleen for consolation, love, affection, and attention. And it didn't bother either of us in the least because all three of them loved both of us, and they understood the entire picture. Kevin already knew about the fertility clinic. Maddy and Mikey knew about Uncle Mike and the fact that he was their donor. They knew it took sperm and an egg to make children, and they called Uncle Mike and Aunt Estefanía by their respective names. Reluctantly, I raised my shirt and showed Kevin my two stretch marks that hadn't gone away. At least, Kathleen had helped me get my flat stomach back. She had been my personal trainer, and other than those two marks, I'm actually in better shape now than I'd ever been in my life.

"Mama B, I miss our old house sometimes," said Maddy.

"I know you do, punkie, but isn't it nice now that everybody has their own bedroom?"

"As if! More than half the time Maddie and Mikey goes to the other's bedroom and slips in bed with the other for the night. When are you going to start sleeping by yourselves?" cackled Kathleen.

Maddie just shrugged her shoulders. She was so cute. She had Kathleen's exact hairdo but such a different personality. She was always so pensive, so lost in thought, as if the entire world was waiting on her for the answer to some intense question. Paying off the mortgage faster on our old house gave us a huge amount of equity when we moved into our new house. It was less than half a mile from our old house, keeping us in roughly the same neighborhood, which made Kathleen very happy. And this time it had a two-car garage *and* a storage shed, so we actually got to park both our vehicles inside. All five bedrooms were upstairs, but ours and the guest room were on one end of the house and the children's bedrooms were on the other end. That made it very nice on those nights when we made love. And I have to say, after almost nine years, the honeymoon was really just beginning. I am so looking forward to what the future has in store for our family!

About HollyAnne Weaver

Ms. Weaver has worked for many years in a scientifically-based career writing technical documents. An avid reader from a very young age, she gradually began writing poetry and fiction, one of her current passions. Growing up, Ms. Weaver was always fascinated with books and the ability of an author to write fiction. A sequence of emails with a close friend led to her writing longer pieces, eventually culminating in her first novel being completed in 2010. Ms. Weaver's main writing focus is on lesbian fiction, although she has projects for mysteries and historical fiction already planned.

LEAVING AFGHANISTAN BEHIND

If you have enjoyed **FURTHER INTO FIRE**
please look for HollyAnne Weaver's novel
LEAVING AFGHANISTAN BEHIND from
Shadoe Publishing, LLC:
We have a chapter here for your enjoyment.

Amelia Gittens, a black female, has the distinct honor of being the first female to be admitted to the US Army's elite group of snipers, fighting in Afghanistan. It doesn't come without its price, though, as she comes back as so many veterans do with post-traumatic stress syndrome complete with major flashbacks. Working as a New York City police officer, she is involved with a suspect shooting. Unfortunately for her, it is the cousin of a major international drug dealer who seeks revenge on her and her partner, as well as the departmental psychiatrist. Amelia responds the only way she knows how, falling back upon her military training to keep her ward safe while the situation is being resolved. The *whole while, she is battling her own inner demons, fighting with herself to keep them at bay, nearly tearing herself apart.*

CHAPTER ONE

"Dispatch, 168. Show me 10-7 at East 46th and Avenue N."
"Roger, 168."
The thought of actually getting thirty minutes to sit and eat was particularly tantalizing to me at this point. It was pretty chilly, even having my Second Chance and my heavy coat. I should have worn long johns underneath everything. What I wouldn't give to be a weatherman. I could be wrong more than forty percent of the time and still get paid like I was a damned genius. Especially with all the forecasts coming from the National Weather Service and purchased software that processed that data.

Then again, even when it was sweltering in the summer and freezing in the winter, I got to be outside and take it all in. You couldn't get me to trade places with one of the desk monkeys at One Police Plaza for all the tea in China. Not a chance! So naturally, when given the choice to eat inside where it was warm, I was stupid enough to take my food out on the sidewalk to a table and eat there. Partially to be outside, and partially to be alone. I'm not a loner, per se. I mean, I have Theresa. She's the love of my life, but I do embrace solitude, for the most part.

"Amelia, sit your ass right back down. You'll catch your death of a cold if you eat outside tonight," said Mama. Make no mistake about it, it was her little restaurant, not the family's. "Are you listening to me?"

"Yes, Mama. I promise I'll come back in for a refill of coffee in just a minute. Let me sit down and take a load off first."

"Take a load off in here, you crazy child!" I laughed under my breath. I felt privileged. She didn't treat just anyone that way. "I don't know why I try with you. You never listen to my advice anyway."

"Not true! Didn't I listen to you when you set me up with Theresa? You were the one that pushed me to ask her out. You practically pushed me in front of a train... or should I say train wreck?" Mama laughed and dismissed me with a wave of her hand. "Come back for that refill or I'll haunt your dreams tonight."

"I don't doubt you will, Mama." I sat my food and coffee on the table and relaxed. As much as I like walking a beat (unlike most cops these days who prefer a cruiser), I do like to sit down and take a load off periodically. I'd no sooner unwrapped my sandwich, when the stupid radio went off.

"All units, vicinity of Flatbush and Quentin, shots fired. 10-32. Approach 10-39. Units in the area respond."

"Dispatch, 168. Show me 10-8 en route, two blocks out. Request 10-78 from 10-60."

I ran like the wind. Shots fired, no other information. Naturally I was the closest respondent. All I wanted was a measly half hour for a meal. Was that too much to ask? I'm not only a marathon runner, I can sprint a 5K. I'm now thirty-one years old, but have never been in better shape. The United States Army took a wiry Flatbush girl, with no experience other than the ability to play basketball, and shaped her into what I am now. I am daily grateful. My mom is so proud! She and papa came from Bermuda with little to their names after paying for college, dragging a few suitcases and me and my sister, Cheryll Anne. We'd all flourished here in the United States, but papa had died the year before I went into the army. I always wished he'd lived just one more year to see me graduate from basic training.

I don't think I ever considered being a lifer. That was brought home to me when I pulled my gauntlet in Southwest Asia. That's where you pull your fifth tour. Supposedly it means that you never have to go back, but that doesn't apply to certain specialties. My best friend growing up, Vam Dho, came back from her sixth deployment in a coffin aboard a C-17. She was Psychological Operations. I did five tours and they wanted me to go again. I would have had to extend my enlistment before I left though, since it ran out about the third week of what would have been a six to nine month deployment.

I was, officially, a military policeman - whatever - I was a sniper!

These things were running through my head while I was beating boots down the sidewalk as fast I could, toward the vicinity of the call. Just as I got there, two men ran out into the street ahead of me. I could clearly see the gun that one of them held, even in the dimly lit street. It was a large automatic pistol, either nickel or stainless steel, with light glinting off it.

"Stop! Police!" I shouted at them, which, of course, both ignored. I pulled my weapon and held it up as I ran, pushing the safety off simultaneously. "Stop! Police!" I repeated, to no avail.

Suddenly the one with the shiny gun turned toward me. I didn't know if the other had a gun, but I definitely knew this one did. I immediately got down into a crouching stance and lowered my weapon at him. "Drop your weapon! Now!" I screamed. Nobody said criminals were smart. I heard a bullet whiz by my head, then heard it strike the brick in the building behind me. I firmly pulled the trigger three times. He dropped. The other man continued to run.

I quickly moved up to the suspect I had shot. He still had a fairly strong pulse, but I knew I'd hit him three times in the gut. I grabbed my radio. "Dispatch, 168, two suspects. One down, three shots. Other suspect is heading south on Hendrickson. Send an ambulance and a squad, 10-18."

"168, 10-4. Stand by." While I waited, I tried to find the wounds through the suspect's coat, after first recovering his pistol and sticking it in the back of my Sam Browne. "168, ambulance and squad dispatched. Ambulance ETA, five to six minutes. Squad ETA, less than two minutes."

"168, 10-4." For a two minute ETA, they sure were quick. The squad fishtailed around the corner and came to a screeching halt about twenty feet from me, their headlights and both spotlights focused on the scene. They killed the siren, but left the flashing lights on.

"I've got this one. The other one ran down Hendrickson on foot. Five ten to six feet, dark hair, light complexion, jeans, dark, heavy coat. Sorry I don't have more!" I yelled out.

The other two officers jumped back in the squad. With a wave from each, they hit the siren again and screeched the tires. I had the suspect on his back. I was trying to apply pressure to his midsection, but he was bleeding too badly. I had a terrible feeling. Even when the bad guy shoots first, even when it's a completely justified shoot, you still feel it. If you don't, you should quit and find a new job.

Finally, the ambulance came lumbering up the street. They pulled up beside me. The driver and passenger hopped out with their bags. The paramedic in the back opened the door from the inside and pulled the stretcher out, joining the other two. There was so much blood! It was all over me, all over the victim, and all over the street. The paramedics took over for me. I stood back, really feeling the lack of food now.

Within four or five minutes, there were four more squads on scene. The first one had gone down the street and found nothing. Another squad close to the site, the patrol sergeant on duty, and the patrol training officer pulled up. The sergeant was there to fill out the reports on weapons discharge and the suspect's condition after a physical confrontation resulting in medical treatment. While the sarge was filling out his paperwork, the second squad was filling out the incident report and had already called in Crime Scene Investigation. The good news was that it was a relatively slow night, and CSI were expected within about fifteen minutes. Even though I was the officer involved, they had to fill out the report for the investigation. My report would be just for the record.

The paramedics had put in a mainline and gone through many pints of blood and plasma, but they couldn't slow the flow of blood enough to transport him. About thirty minutes into it, they pulled the parachute cord and bailed. They'd have to wait for CSI before they could leave, but in the meantime it took them a good twenty minutes to get everything squared away.

The paramedics had begun cleaning me up and making sure that I had no injuries. My right knee was a little out of sorts from all the pounding on the pavement getting over here, plus the chase... I'm not twenty-one any more. They gave me some naproxen for that, along with a twenty-four ounce bottle of water with added electrolytes to keep me hydrated. I thanked them for their help. They'd also given me a couple of Mylar blankets to wrap up in and let me sit in the back of the ambulance until I could get some replacement clothes. My shirt and coat were soaked with blood, but at least it was off my hands and arms now.

The back of the ambulance opened and the sarge and the reporting officer got in, shutting the door behind them. "Amelia, from what I've gathered already, it was a good, clean shoot. No worries there. Glen here is going to drive you over to the precinct so that you can finish your report while it's still fresh in your head. Then we're going to kick you loose, with pay of course, and you'll have to drive a desk for a few days until we get the official okay from 1PP." He handed me the business card of the head doctor, as required by departmental regulations. "Dr. Feynman is the duty shrink for this week. Call her! Let her do her job! Even if you feel fine. I'm not kidding!"

"No need to shout, Timmy. I heard you the first time."

"I could bust you for insubordination. Not for not using my rank, but for calling me Timmy instead of Tim. For God's sake, Amelia, you're not my parents. I could get away with kicking your ass," he said playfully, punching me in the arm. "I'm going to head home now. I've been on duty since six thirty this morning. Call Dr. Feynman. Promise me."

"I promise, Sarge. Go on home to Rita. Glen will take care of me."

"Good night, you two."

"Good night, Sarge," Glen and I said in unison.

Glen looked me right in the eyes. "Does this bring anything back? I have never discharged my weapon, but I've drawn it, and it takes me back."

✦ HOLLYANNE WEAVER ✦

Glen was in my unit at the same time, but we always deployed opposite each other, so we never met until we joined the force at the NYPD. On paper, we were the XVIII Airborne Corps, 16th MP Brigade, 91st MP Battalion, 32nd MP Company out of Fort Bragg. When we were deployed, we became the 10th Mountain Division, 1st Brigade, 10th Military Police Battalion, 1st Platoon. Officially you had to be an infantryman, a Special Forces member, a Stryker, or a cavalry scout, but since women weren't allowed in those jobs, they allowed me to be selected from an MP unit that was embedded in an infantry division. But then, in those blurred lines that sometimes present themselves, life wasn't what it seemed.

I said nothing. He helped me into the squad he was driving and took me back to the precinct. I had a couple of spare shirts in my locker and he managed to find me a couple of hoodies to put on. They were both oversized for me, so I had no problem getting them on. I put my beat cap in my locker and picked up a snapback and threw it on. I also got my chain out and put my ID on it so that I could be identified throughout the building. After I finished filling out my report, Glen, who was about ready for his coffee break, came in where I was set up and took my reports to turn in. Then he picked up the phone, slammed it against the desk in front of me, picked up the handset, and shoved it in my face.

"I'll do it."

"When."

"Later. I promise."

"You'll do it now!"

I sighed, pulling out the card for Dr. Feynman. I punched the numbers into the phone as Glen was leaving the office, gently pulling the door shut behind him.

"This is Elizabeth Feynman. May I help you?"

"Dr. Feynman. This is Officer Amelia Gittens. I was just… involved in a suspect shooting." Dr. Feynman immediately lost the sound of sleepiness in her voice.

"Amelia, are you there?"

"Yeah. Look, I can call you tomorrow if you'd like. It's almost midnight now."

"Which precinct are you at right now?"

"67th Flatbush."

"Give me twenty-five minutes. I'll be right there."

"Really, I can do this tomorrow."

LEAVING AFGHANISTAN BEHIND

"Nonsense. The sooner we do this, the better it will be. See you in a few. Just don't make fun of me without makeup," she laughed. I tried to laugh, but it didn't come.

Next, I pulled out my cell phone. "Hi, baby. How are you tonight?"

"Knowing you're going to be walking in that door in less than an hour, how could I not be perfect?"

"About that... I'm... uh... going to be a little late. I've got to hang out here at the precinct for a while. I'm waiting on the departmental psychiatrist to have an hour visit with me before I can leave, and she won't be here for about half an hour. Then I have to get a ride home. They won't let me drive tonight."

"Baby! What's wrong? Are you all right? Did you get hurt?"

"No, I'm fine actually. It was just... well, you're going to hear about it anyway. I was involved in a shooting tonight."

"But you're fine, right? Tell me you're fine."

"Yeah, I'm just fine. I had a suspect shoot at me. He missed. I didn't."

"...So, you shot him? Or her? Or whatever?"

"Yeah. I shot him three times. The ambulance couldn't even get him stable enough to transport."

"Baby girl, are you sure you're okay?"

"I'll be fine. I don't technically have to see the shrink tonight, but I won't be allowed to do anything without talking to one of them, so I might as well get it over with. I'll see you in a couple of hours. I just wanted to let you know I'd be late. Scratch Ferdinand for me. See you in a while. Love you."

"I love you too, baby. So much."

Theresa Biancardi was almost an empath, she cared so much. Not just about me, about everybody really, but especially towards me. Her family had some trouble getting used to me. Not because I'm black, but because of my sounds-sort-of-British-but-not-quite accent.

Finally, the doctor showed up. "Hello, Officer Gittens. I'm Elizabeth Feynman. Please, let's find some place a little more conducive to a chat than this office." We found a lounge area, where she took out a large sticky note and put it on the door. She wrote on it with a big marker, 'IN USE'. "Please, come in. Sit down and make yourself comfortable."

We both got seated, but neither of us spoke, initially. I understood quickly, she was waiting for me to go first in order to judge my condition. I played it coy for a few minutes before finally deciding to speak, "So when you go out on one these little ventures, do you jump on the departmental database and do a quick dossier scan before coming out, or something like that?"

"Or something like that," she responded.

"So you already know what I did before joining the NYPD. Right?"

"You were an MP in the army."

"Does my quick record show what my TDYs were?"

"All I know is that you were in the army as an MP for thirteen and a half years, and that you retired honorably as a Sergeant First Class. It takes an absolute minimum of twelve and a half years to make SFC and yet you achieved that grade and functioned there for some time. It also says that you have a Bronze Star with two oak leaf clusters and two Vs, Global War on Terrorism medal with three clusters, a Commendation Medal with oak leaf cluster, Afghanistan Campaign medal with three clusters, Distinguished Service Medal, Good Conduct Medal, two Purple Hearts, Army Achievement Medal twice, and a Combat Infantry Badge. Christ! That's only the first quarter or so of the alphabet. And that's only medals, not to mention ribbons and awards. It doesn't say why, it just says that you have them. If you don't mind my asking, what were the extent of your wounds?"

I stood up from my chair, pulled my tee shirt up and my sweat bottoms down about four inches. That let her see the scars from four bullet holes. "Dr. Feynman, I rarely performed MP duties in the army."

"Being from an enemy weapon, those would be thirty caliber wounds, correct?"

I nodded my head at her. I was impressed that she knew the difference and the implications that went along with them.

"So what did you do?"

"I was a sniper. I was already in the 10th Mountain Division, firmly embedded in Afghanistan, but worked primarily in the forward combat brigades. I still wore my MP insignias, in addition to the ones for the unit I worked with. That's what I did for about eighty percent of my time, both at home and deployed. My rotations home were always short, and my deployments always long."

"Well, that explains the CIB. I wondered about that. Most MPs don't get those."

"You do if you're working in a forward area, actually. Glen Parsons, the officer that wrote up my incident tonight, was in my unit at the same time. Never met him until we both started working here. Sort of funny. He has a Silver Star, a Commendation Medal, and a CIB, but he wasn't a sniper."

"Let's talk about being sniper a little bit before we move on. Do you have any confirmed kills?"

"Yes."

"Do you know how many?"

"Yes."

"Would you mind sharing that with me?"

"Yes."

"Amelia, I'm not the enemy here, I'm your friend. I'm not going to be asked to testify at your review board. In fact, I'm prohibited by both licensure and law (not to mention the union), from doing so. I'm just trying to get a baseline for you. The more I know, the more I can help you."

"Who says I need help?"

"That was poorly worded. How about the more I know, the more I can make myself available to you for whatever support I can give? Is that better?"

"Much." I paused for a couple of minutes. What the hell. "Seventeen confirmed, thirty-one suspected."

"And how do you feel about that, after the fact? Not at that moment, but now."

"Whatever."

"Does it bother you? Do you ever have nightmares? Have you ever been diagnosed with PTSD, even mild?"

"Yes, yes, and yes."

"Okay. Let's move on to tonight. What happened?"

"I'm a beat cop. I responded to a call. I gave chase to two suspects. One had a gun that was easy to see, even at night. Shiny. Forty-five caliber. I identified myself twice and gave them warning to stop. Both suspects failed to respond. Shortly after that, the suspect with the gun fired one round that missed me. I did hear the bullet whiz by, so it must have been fairly close. I fired three rounds into the suspect. Guaranteed to immobilize, but not overkill. The other suspect ran away. I radioed in the situation to dispatch and immediately cleared the suspect's weapon and begin giving him first aid as best I could. The paramedics weren't able to save him."

"How did it make you feel, hearing the bullet go by you?"

"I didn't particularly have an opinion one way or another about it, ma'am."

"Please, no need for ma'am. You can call me Elizabeth if you like."

"Actually, I'd prefer Dr. Feynman."

"That's okay as well. So you didn't get upset? Angry? Scared? Nothing particular regarding being shot at?"

"No, but it was because of that I returned fire. I would never have shot first. I would have let them escape and evade before shooting first."

"Departmental policy does give you circumstances where you not only should, but are required to, shoot first if there is a safety issue for the public or yourself."

"Are you going to report me for what I just said, ma'am?"

"No, of course not. I wish I could get you to understand that I represent your interests here, nobody else's. I tell you what, I want some time to review my notes, develop a little plan of action if you will, for you to follow. We'll talk again."

"How often will I have to report to you before returning to duty?"

"Officer Gittens, I really want to see you again. At least a few times. Maybe three or four if you would consent, but as far as I'm concerned, I'll sign off for you tomorrow. I'll have your notice of record included in your jacket to go to the review board, to allow them to rest assured. Okay?"

"Thank you, ma'am."

"On one condition…"

"What's that?"

"Just once, say it. Say Elizabeth. Then I promise you, I'll clear you," she smiled.

I managed to smile back at her, even if I didn't mean it wholeheartedly. I stood up from my chair and stared her down for a minute. I extended my hand to her and said, "Elizabeth. Thank you."

As she shook my hand, she said, "You're welcome. Now was that so hard?"

"No, ma'am." We both broke out laughing then. A long, hard, belly laugh. It broke the tension tremendously. That alone made me feel better than everything else did. There was something about talking to a shrink. I kept having to do it on active duty, and with the VA for the two or three years after I got out because I had PTSD. The day you go in and talk to them, and even the day after, you feel like crud. Then you get better, better than if you hadn't gone. Maybe it was just stirring everything up that created that feeling.

Since Elizabeth was going my way, she offered to give me a ride home. I took her up on it. I thanked her again as I closed the car door and waved goodbye. I went to the door and was fumbling with the lock and my key, when Theresa yanked it open. She grabbed my hoody and jerked me inside. "Hi, baby girl. How are you doing?"

"I'm fine," was about all I could muster.

"Are you sure?"

"Yeah. I'm fine."

"Do you maybe want a little *happy time* tonight?" she asked.

"Not really. I just want a hot shower and to go to bed."

"Are you sure?" she asked, grabbing the hands on my hips, her thumbs tickling me playfully.

"I'm sure," I said, pulling her hand away. "Let me take a shower, and then we'll cuddle up together in bed. Would that be okay for tonight?"

"No problem."

"Are you disappointed?"

"Baby, I just want to do everything I can to make you as happy as I can tonight. You've had the shittiest of all possible nights, I suspect. I'll do anything, not do anything, you just tell me what you need and I'll make it so. I'll even get you a hooker if it helps," she joked.

"Now that sounds pretty darn good. The thing is, my girlfriend, she's sort of the jealous type. She doesn't snoop my email or anything like that, but I hardly think she'd take kindly to my fooling around with another chick," I cracked back at her, jokingly.

"You got that shit right! She's a whack, totally wicked bitch when it comes to that. I don't see what you'd want in another woman anyway. After all, she's so cute, and adorable, and funny, and loving…"

"Or so she thinks," I said with a grin.

"But she loves you. More than anything in the world."

"Next time you see her? Tell her that I was the one who fell in love first. I was the one who told her first, and I was the one who asked her to marry me first…"

"What?"

"You heard me. Tell her that I was the one who asked her to marry me first."

"So you're…" she started, shaking her head. "You're asking me to marry you?"

"I was thinking of the right way to tell you. I've been carrying this damn thing around with me for three days at work, thinking about it while I was out pounding the pavement. Usually, I'm pretty good at presenting myself, but this one was different." I got down on the floor on one knee, in front of the couch where she was sitting, and pulled out the ring box. "Theresa Rosanna Biancardi, will you marry me, and live with me, and have babies with me, for the rest of my life?"

She launched herself up and on me, with her arms around my neck, and began crying uncontrollably. Finally she stepped back, tears still flowing, and put her hand out so I could put the ring on her finger. It was a little difficult because she kept shaking her hand up and down. Finally, I took my left hand and grabbed her thumb to hold her hand in place, and used my right hand to slide the ring up. She kept her hand flat to see what it looked like on her. Still, she cried and cried. I wrapped her arms around my neck again, and I encircled her waist and picked her off the floor. I carried her like that into the bathroom, then put her down. She took off her night shirt and her underwear, then reached in to turn on the water in the shower. I took my clothes off and made a little pile on the floor. She stepped in first, then held out her hand, beckoning me. I took her hand, then stepped in beside her. Her tears were gone and now she was simply beaming at me with those crystal clear, blue grey eyes, so common in the north of her country of origin. We washed each other, rinsed each other, dried each other, and dressed each other. Then we crawled beneath the covers and snuggled in tightly. We were both asleep in minutes. Unfortunately, I didn't stay there.

End Sample Chapter of LEAVING AFGHANISTAN BEHIND
For more go to www.Shadoepublishing.com to purchase
the complete book or for many other delightful offerings.

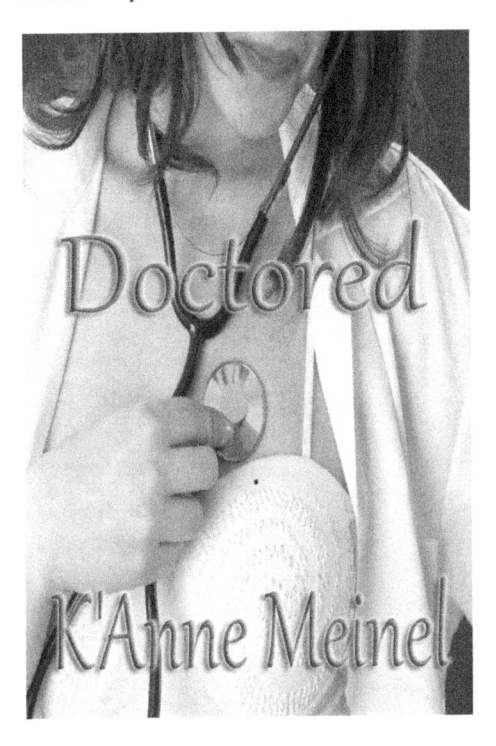

~ Because a publisher should stand behind their authors~

A brilliant child protégée, she dreams of becoming a doctor and a surgeon...and accomplishes her goals. Unfortunately, her youth and round, child-like face work against her. No matter how skilled she becomes, how knowledgeable, the old school, male-dominated medical hierarchy wants to keep her in 'her place.'

Deanna has worked hard to become an expert in her chosen field, but few believe this 'child' capable. Specializing in infectious diseases, she travels the world—from the States to Europe to South America—honing her skills before winding up in Africa where her skills are desperately needed.

Meeting a nurse by the name of Madison MacGregor, she finds they share an insatiable curiosity and a love of helping others, but falling in love was not what she intended. Later, when she loses Maddie to a misunderstanding, she is haunted by the one that got away...

Ten years have passed and both the doctor and nurse have moved on with their lives, but fate intervenes when they find themselves working at the same hospital. Their friendship is revived...can their love be rekindled? Will the past haunt them or bring them closer? Will the secrets that both harbor keep them from realizing a future together?

www.shadoepublishing.com

~ *Because a publisher should stand behind their authors~*

THE Path Not Chosen

Q.C. MASTERS

What do you do when you meet someone who changes everything you know about love and passion?

Paige Harlow is a good girl. She's always known where she was going in life: top grades, an ivy league school, a medical degree, regular church attendance, and a happy marriage to a man. So falling in love with her gorgeous roommate and best friend Alyssa Torres is no small crisis. Alyssa is chasing demons of her own, a medical condition that makes her an outcast and a family dysfunctional to the point of disintegration make her a questionable choice for any stable relationship. But Paige's heart is no longer her own. She must now battle the prejudices of her family, friends, and church and come to peace with her new sexuality before she can hope to win the affections of the woman of her dreams. But will love be enough?

www.shadoepublishing.com

~ Because a publisher should stand behind their authors~

As I watch the wormhole start to close, I make one last desperate plea...
"Please? Please don't make me do this?" I whisper.
"You're almost out of time, Lily. Please, just let go?"
I look down at the control panel. I know what I have to do.

Lilith Madison is captain of the Phoenix, a spaceship filled with an elite crew and travelling through the Delta Gamma Quadrant. Their mission is mankind's last hope for survival.

But there is a killer on board. One who kills without leaving a trace and seems intent on making sure their mission fails. With the ship falling apart and her crew being ruthlessly picked off one by one, Lilith must choose who to trust while tracking down the killer before it's too late.

"A suspenseful...exciting...thrilling whodunit adventure in space...discover the shocking truth about what's really happening on the Phoenix" (Clarion)

www.shadoepublishing.com

~ *Because a publisher should stand behind their authors~*

FAST LANE
JENNIS SLAUGHTER
A.D. CAMPBELL

In the male dominated sport of Formula 1 racing, Samantha 'Sam' Dupree is struggling to make her mark against the boys. She hears about a driver who is making a name for herself in NASCAR and goes to check her out. Little does she know that she's in for the race of her heart.

Addison McCloud wants nothing more than to drive. She doesn't care about fame or fortune; she just wants to be fast enough to get herself and her family away from her abusive father. Meeting Sam changes her world and revs her life into overdrive.

When the two women meet, sparks fly like the race cars that they drive. Will they be able to steer their relationship into something more and win the race, or will their families make them crash and burn? The boys of Formula 1 are going to learn that Southern girls are a force to be reckoned with.

www.shadoepublishing.com

~ *Because a publisher should stand behind their authors~*

FRANKIE

PRUDENCE MACLEOD
IN COLLABORATION WITH
CRYSTIANNA CRAWFORD

    Carrie flees from the demons of her present, trying to protect the ones she loves.

    Frankie hides from the demons of her past, and the memory of loved ones she failed to protect.

    A modern day princess thrown to the wolves, Carrie's only hope is the rancher who had spent the better part of a decade in self imposed, near total, isolation. Frankie's history of losing those she tries to save haunts her, but this madman threatens her home, her livestock, her sanctuary. She knows she can't do it alone, has she still got enough support from her oldest friends?

www.shadoepublishing.com

~ Because a publisher should stand behind their authors~

RIDING THE RAINBOW
GENTA SEBASTIAN

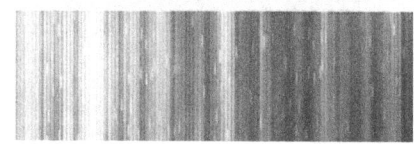

A Children's Novel for ages 8-11

Horse crazy Lily, eleven years old with two out-loud-and-proud mothers, is plump and clumsy. Her mothers say she's too young to ride horses, she can't seem to get anything right in class, and bullies torment her on the playground. Alone and lonely, how will she ever survive the mean girls of Hardyvale Elementary's fifth-grade?

Across the room Clara sits still as a statue, never volunteering or raising her hand. To avoid the bullying that is Lily's daily life she answers only in a whisper with her head down, desperate to keep her family's secret that she has two fathers.

Then one day Clara makes a brave move that changes the girls' lives forever. She passes a note to Lily asking to meet secretly at lunch time. As they share cupcakes she explains about her in-the-closet dads. Both girls are relieved to finally have a friend, especially one who understands about living in a rainbow family.

Life gets better. As their friendship deepens and their families grow close, their circle of friends expand. The girls even volunteer together at the local animal shelter. Everything is great, until old lies and blackmail catch up with them. Can Lily and her mothers rescue Clara's family from disaster? Or will Lily lose her first and best friend?

www.shadoepublishing.com

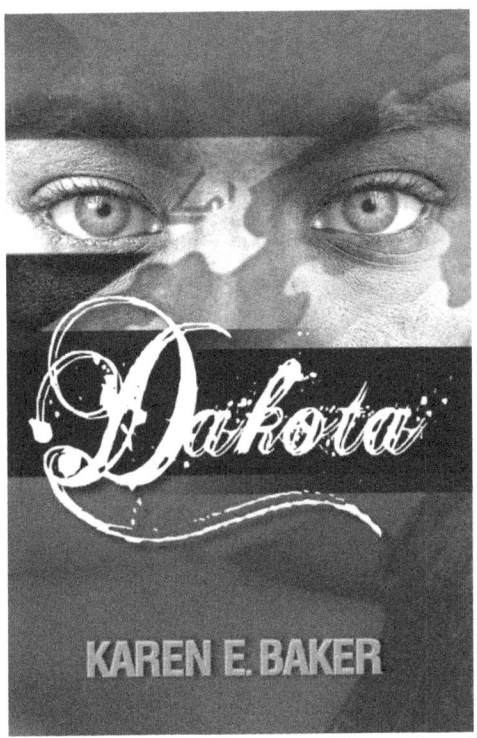

~ Because a publisher should stand behind their authors~

When U.S. Marine Dakota McKnight returned home from her third tour in Operation Iraqi Freedom, she carried more baggage than the gear and dress blues she had deployed with. A vicious rocket-propelled grenade attack on her base left her best friend dead and Dakota physically and emotionally wounded. The marine who once carried herself with purpose and confidence, has returned broken and haunted by the horrors of war. When she returns to the civilian world, life is not easy, but with the help of her therapist, Janie, she is barely managing to hold her life together...then she meets Beth.

Beth Kendrick is an American history college professor. She is as straight-laced as they come, until Dakota enters her life, that is. Will her children understand what she is going through? Will she take a chance on the broken marine or decide to wait for the perfect someone to come along?

Time is on your side, they say, unless there is a dark, sinister evil at work. Is their love strong enough to hold these two people together? Will the love of a good woman help Dakota find the path to recovery? Or is she doomed to a life of inner turmoil and destruction that knows no end?

www.shadoepublishing.com

*If you have enjoyed this book and the others listed here Shadoe Publishing, LLC is always looking for authors. Please check out our website @ www.shadoepublishing.com
For information or to contact us @
shadoepublishing@gmail.com.*

We may be able to help you make your dreams of becoming a published author come true.

Made in the USA
Middletown, DE
27 August 2019